Second-best
BRIDE

Other Five Star Titles
by Ruth Glover:

The Shining Light
Bitter Thistle, Sweet Rose
Turn Northward, Love

Second-best
BRIDE

Ruth Glover

Five Star • Waterville, Maine

Published in 2004 in conjunction with Beacon Hill Press
of Kansas City.

The text of this edition is unabridged.

Set in 11 pt. Plantin by Elena Picard.

Printed in the United States on permanent paper.

Library of Congress Cataloging-in-Publication Data

Glover, Ruth.
    Second-best bride / Ruth Glover.
        p. cm.—(The wild rose series ; bk. 5)
     ISBN 1-59414-055-3 (hc : alk. paper)
       1. Wildrose (Sask.)—Fiction. 2. Women pioneers—
Fiction. I. Title.
    PS3557.L678S4 2004
    813'.54—dc21   2003053917

Second-best
BRIDE

1

"This bicycle hooliganism," rapped the stern admonition from the pulpit, "is a sign of the times!"

The preacher's timing was perfect. Even as he spoke, local members of the Wheelman's Association—about 50 of them—tootled past the church, and every eye in the congregation turned to watch them, some with disapproval, some with envy.

That Meg Shaw's response to the high-flying group was one of envy was not because she yearned for a bicycle. Meg's heart yearned for the *freedom* the bicyclists so clearly depicted. Faint laughter could be heard between the speaker's remarks, and the fresh summer breeze made streamers of the ribbons on the small, mostly flat straw hats worn by two or three of the girls of the group.

Meg's sister, Marlys, sitting by her side and watching the pedalers critically, hissed in Meg's ear, "Some of them are wearing the *wrong hat!* Any simpleton knows proper protocol calls for a little cap with a tiny peak or brim!"

And Marlys should know. In her own suit with its bolero cape and very full taffeta-lined skirt bound with velvet, she was, as always, a fashion plate. Its color—blue—exactly matched her eyes; its collar and lapels were appliquéd and elegantly embroidered, and the cape itself had four rows of soutache all around it. And it was topped, of course, with the proper hat. It was made of fancy rough straw, trimmed with a plume finished with a large rosette of dotted net on the right and three loops of net held by a large bunch of flowers on the left. Turned up saucily in back, it revealed Marlys's piled golden curls to advantage.

Meg's suit paled in comparison. Anyone else might have felt like a sparrow sitting beside a peacock, but not Meg. She had had a lifetime of evaluating herself and her sister and was content to be who and what she was.

"Marlys," Harley, their brother, said once, "is a gaud; Meggie is a romp," and thought he paid them each a compliment. Neither Marlys nor Meg had quite known what he meant and so the insult or compliment, whichever it was, was allowed to pass.

Checking the dictionary later, Meg decided she would settle for *romp*. *Gaud* meant a trinket or ornament and had no appeal for Meg. *Romp* she accepted—but only because that was what Harley remembered of her. Until recently Harley had not seen his sisters for five years. Now, Meg felt, while she did indeed enjoy life, she had learned a little decorum. Harley would change his mind about her. But about Marlys? Probably not.

Before the members of the bicycle club passed from sight, Meg looked with fresh interest at the ladies of the group, prompted no doubt by her sister's observation.

It wasn't simple to go bicycling. The experience called for its own special outfit. After all, one couldn't just leap astride a machine and pedal off! Every female's outfit, Meg knew, consisted of five pieces: the natty little cap mentioned by Marlys, a short jacket (which, of course, had to have the huge leg-of-mutton sleeves now popular on all suits), a skirt shortened a scandalous eight or so inches, leggings that buttoned snugly up the calf, and—that item that had the whole country abuzz—bloomers. Hidden somewhere under the full skirt, the bloomers nevertheless flashed into sight with the vigorous pedaling sometimes engaged in.

All in all, the scene was freedom personified to a city-bred and -raised girl. Still, it wasn't a bicycle Meg longed for; they had been around, in one developing stage or another, for almost a hundred years. Only recently, however, had they become comfortable; she watched the frolicsome gaggle of riders and thought, *I'd rather be riding in a buckboard!*

Sitting sedately beside her sister and evaluating not only Marlys's outfit but also those of the pedalers, her heart's cry was, *I'd rather have a gingham gown and a sunbonnet!*

In the meantime, the preacher's message was eliciting some murmured amens and nodded heads.

" 'In the last days perilous times shall come,' " the pastor reminded his flock and warned against being "lovers of pleasure more than lovers of God." And he enlarged on a problem about which they were all aware—the young bicycle-riding "hooligans" who rode rampant through gardens and over lawns, frightened horses and put buggies to flight, ran down chicken or child alike in their exuberance, terrorizing the neighborhood.

And then there was the problem of desecrating the Sabbath. As proof, the careless, carefree group jaunted past, headed for the country and a day of release from 10-hour days in the workforce. And, because of the comfortable saddle and other features, such as the dropped frame, giving women their own machine, females were as involved as males.

Harley had looked into the possibility of owning a bicycle, hoping to ride it to work. But Wilda, his wife, had warned, "It's the first downward step, Harley!"

Because of Harley's squelched interest, they all knew the intimate details of the bicycle. The bicycle had evolved from a sort of hobbyhorse on wheels to the "Bone Shaker" velocipede to the monstrosity with its five-foot front wheel, so difficult to mount that one had to use a horse block, to the pneumatic tire, ball bearings, adjustable handlebars, and coaster brakes now available.

But it was the seat or "saddle" that made all the difference, Harley said and pointed out to his womenfolk the choices: the hygienic or racing saddle, the messenger hygienic (unequaled for comfort), or the plew or the American racing saddle.

"Racing! I'm sure!" Wilda had snorted. "And the expense of the bicycle would be just the beginning, Harley! Look at the gadgets!"

She was right, of course. A person could spend a fortune on gadgetry. Tool bags, special lunch boxes shaped to fit the wheel, bicycle pumps, pedals (for gents a "rat trap pattern thoroughly dustproof and will withstand all hard usage"; for ladies "a very light and beautiful pedal that can be changed to a rat trap if so desired"). And then there was the bell that "rings loud and clear; won't wake the dead, but comes as near it as any of them"; the siren whistle that "produces any kind of a sound, from a groan to an unearthly shriek, at the will of the operator." There were bicycle locks, pocket-sized oilers, folding parcel carriers, toe clips and spoke grips, mudguards, lamps, and of course repair kits. It was mind-boggling.

"I can see a great deal of sense in this cyclists' cape," Harley had said wistfully. " 'It forms,' " he read, " 'an umbrella-like shape and protects the rider from the rain.' "

"And then, Harley," Wilda pointed out while Marlys and

Meg listened, fascinated, to this marital skirmish, "you'd have to have special bicycling knickers," and Wilda's amused eyebrow was more than her husband could stand.

"Are you saying," he said, frostily, "that my calves are less than presentable?"

"Oh, Harley," Wilda said placatingly, "it's not just the knickers! It's those silly hose supporters—that belt that goes around the waist, those elastic straps with the fasteners to attach to the hose you would have to wear."

"I suppose," Harley had said, sighing and laying aside the advertisement they had been studying, "I'll just continue riding the cars. But," he couldn't help but add cunningly, "it does cost a nickel each way. That would all count up on the cost of the bike's purchase."

But Wilda was not to be enticed.

Now, with the fast-flying cyclists hurtling past the church window, Meg craned her head for one last glimpse of their dizzying taste of independence. As usual, she breathed shallowly because of the constrictions of her wasp-waisted "toilette," which made it difficult to heave a massive sigh. But even the small sigh that escaped her caused her wide sleeve to brush against her sister's equally wide sleeve. Marlys frowned, and Meg obligingly moved over, being well accustomed to her sister's correction and finding it simpler to cooperate than to raise an objection.

Tuning out the continuing tirade against the "implement of Satan," Meg fell into a reverie, a familiar reverie.

In it she rode in a buckboard (or, at times, in her wildest imagining, *astride* a horse) across the stretching prairie. She could almost feel her hair blow free of the constricting pins needed to keep it piled properly. She exulted in the gingham dress billowing in the wind; her hands, browned by the sun, had a firm grip on taut reins. The mile-devouring stride brought her nearer and nearer to . . .

Even in her dreams Meg had trouble imagining the house of her destination as a soddy. But whatever the abode, she always knew it was indeed *home,* a home of her very own after years of living in England with an elderly aunt and several months with her brother, Harley, in Toronto, Canada.

Today, as always, rather than the vistas of the prairie, reality for Meg was a window-sized view of Toronto that, though new and crude in some ways, was not a great deal different from the smoky city she and Marlys had left when Harley had written to say that he was, at last, in a position to have his sisters live with him.

What a day of departure that had been! Marlys reluctant to leave friends and comfort and security for the unknown; Meg eager to embrace whatever the new land had to offer.

After one night in a hotel in Liverpool, they had boarded the *Lake Manitoba* and set sail for their new life. Landing at St. John, New Brunswick, they had proceeded westward by train.

But not far enough westward!

Words could never describe the sick disappointment Meg had felt when she realized their final destination was still hundreds of miles from the place that—never having seen it—tugged at her heart.

She had looked around at the city—at Harley dapper in his cassimere suit, his stiff black derby, his fine polished cane in his hand, and his pointed patent leather oxfords on his feet—and grieved that they weren't overalls, a pitchfork, and two-buckle plow shoes!

How could he contentedly fit into the old life in the new place! It seemed incredible to Meg.

The entire world knew about the vast Northwest Territory and its offer of free land. The Honorable Clifford Sifton, minister of the interior, had seen to that. Charged with the responsibility of peopling its plains and determined to turn the West into the nation's breadbasket, he had skillfully and successfully advertised to recruit homesteaders.

In Great Britain, where Meg and Marlys waited, a fever spread to claim land, with almost irresistible appeal to people whose lives had been spent in subjection to lord and landlord for centuries. With others, Harley had already taken ship for the distant continent, with the promise to send for his sisters as soon as he could.

But Harley had looked for, and found, employment in Toronto, Ontario. Here, in the piano manufactory of one Gerhard Heintzman, he spent his days as humdrum, Meg was certain, as his mill work had been in England. He had, to her thinking, simply exchanged one area for another; his lifestyle remained much the same.

Except that, along the way, Harley had acquired a wife. He and Wilda had married. Then two children, Danny and Daisy, had come along to bless the union as well as delay once more the arrival of Marlys and Meg.

That Harley, with such an opportunity, was not among the land seekers! But Harley had said, "I'm a city man, Meg. Besides, I have a wife and children now. Take them off to those uncertain prairies? Not likely! Aside from the usual severe problems, don't you know the last few years have seen a terrible drought on the prairies?"

He was right. As dust gathered and blew on the grassy plains, districts that were beginning to become settled had been deserted and farmers had left by the thousands. The prairies, once so impelling and compelling, quickly lost their appeal to people whose main interest was keeping body and soul together.

So the wind blew and the land shifted, and dreams whirled over the horizon, and men, only flesh and blood after all and not the gods they had begun to feel, silently closed the doors to their soddies and shacks, packed their few belongings, and escaped. One of them, as much in earnestness as in jest, said, "The two books of the Old Testament that describe the situation are Lamentations and Exodus."

But the exodus was over. Everything was changing. The prairies were producing abundantly again. Once again the cry "Free land!" was drawing the land-hungry to the Northwest. The mood in the land was confident, enthusiastic.

And it would have been so canny, Meg thought, to have picked up land that was partially developed when it was there, empty, for the taking. That some men had been far-sighted enough she knew. As evidence of this, a manly figure sat in the Ferguson pew across the aisle from the Shaw entourage (Harley, Wilda, Danny, Daisy, Marlys, and Meg).

Though a stranger to Meg, she knew who he was. His sister, Becky, seated proudly at his side, was Meg's friend.

"My brother is coming home," she had told Meg, "that is, *one* of my brothers. They both went West about four years ago."

West, but not to the prairies, Meg was surprised to hear. The bush country, north of the prairies and south of the boreal forests, was their choice.

"Still just as cold, I suppose," Becky had said, "but without the open sweeps that make for such terrible blizzards. And they have lots of wood to burn, that's for sure. And they don't build soddies, having plenty of trees."

Just what had brought this particular Ferguson brother home, Meg didn't know. But Becky had gigglingly hinted that it might be to find a wife.

"There's a great lack of women out there," she had said, adding thoughtfully, "I might just get my brother to take me back with him!"

But Becky Ferguson was only 15, and she, Meg, was almost 18. Eighteen and sadly discontented with life in Toronto. Here, she thought restlessly, life proceeded much the same as in England. The well-to-do lived in big turreted homes, crowded with bric-a-brac and smothered in drapery. And in them the poor worked for small wages and went home to tenements full of misery, want, and sickness.

In spite of the Factory Act of 1891, 13-year-olds still worked 60-hour weeks in mills and refineries. Younger children sewed at home, working far into the night hours. Some begged on the streets; some, Meg had seen with horror, plied unspeakable professions in the dark corners of the city to make a living. The more enterprising sold apples, shined shoes, peddled papers. Women worked in factories where gas irons leaked day in and day out, breathing the unhealthy effluence continually. Their homes had no plumbing; thousands of outhouses gave off noxious fumes and contaminated the drinking water. Adults died regularly from tuberculosis; diphtheria was the merciless killer of children.

And still the immigrants poured in and now, once again, headed West. Seeking new horizons, a beginning, escaping persecution, longing for a place of their own— these were a few of the reasons that drove men and women from the known to the unknown. They were a courageous group.

And Meg felt like one of them! To be so limited, so hampered, and all because she was a female. Feeling like a crusader on the inside, her womanliness branded her unfit.

There had to be a way! The raw bustlings of Toronto were too sophisticated for Meg Shaw!

But Harley—content with his job, his wife, his life, his future—thought the new world, even in Toronto, was challenging.

"Just listen to this," he had said one night over the evening paper while the rest of his family finished their pudding. "There's talk that we will eventually have a union with our neighbor to the south. Then watch the economy boom! It should mean a greater outlet for our player pianos, for one thing."

Pianos! Meg's pudding turned sour to her taste.

Not getting the attention of his womenfolk with news of the economy, Harley had said, "This here is about Mrs. Bloomer's bifurcated nether garment," and got their curious glances. Wilda stopped wiping mashed potatoes from Danny's face, Marlys looked up from the society page, and Meg left off her daydreaming.

"This editorial says, 'The female who wears them is a fright.' What do you think of that, eh?" Harley, who loved a debate, peered around the edge of his paper, his eyes twinkling with anticipation.

Wilda's lips had pinched; Marlys looked bored; Meg, who longed for freedom, considered the idea of the divided garment. Not for the first time she decided, "They would be perfect for riding horses."

Disappointed, Harley returned to his reading. Shortly, however, he guffawed loudly; the women of his household again forsook individual thoughts to hear him out.

"What's so funny?" Wilda wanted to know.

"This writer says that bloomers reveal 'the most shapeless lot of legs ever seen outside a butcher shop.' "

Harley was going too far! Wilda took her responsibility

16

to her younger sisters-in-law seriously. Thank goodness Daisy was too young to be influenced by such unbridled speech!

"Harley!" she said, reproachfully.

Harley was quick to offer an apology. "I'm sorry, my dear. I should have substituted 'limbs.' "

Wilda was somewhat mollified by her husband's correction of the offending word; Marlys and Meg grinned at each other.

Now, in church, recalling the conversation, and with the last female bicyclist and her pumping "limbs" disappearing in a cloud of dust, Meg wondered: *Did one call a cow's leg a limb?*

The Ferguson man, a farmer, would know all about cows and their appendages. Meg wondered how he might react if, at the dinner table, she should say, "Please pass the limb of lamb."

This line of thought started a hysterical eruption, which she covered quickly by a cough. Even so, Marlys was disturbed. Putting a gloved finger to her pink lips, she whispered, with a severe frown wrinkling her fair brow, "SH!"

Come to think of it, the Ferguson man would know a great deal more about animals than what to call their body parts. Meg looked thoughtfully across the aisle. Perhaps aware of her gaze, perhaps having heard her outbreak, the Ferguson man chose that moment to turn and look at her. His eyes, in that brief moment, were startling in their light color—almost a silvery gray. His face, square and strong, was the brown of a northwoodsman. Altogether a good-looking man.

And he had come to Toronto, according to Becky, to find a wife. And he came—not from the prairies—but from the bush country. A remote district, Becky had reported, called Wildrose. In the heart of a strip of parkland in Saskatchewan.

Meg knew little or nothing about the bush. But the names sang in her mind . . . or perhaps her heart.

Saskatchewan: On the map, Meg had traced the river that sprawled like a shaky Y from the Snow Dome in the Columbia Icefields, separating into north and south branches and called, by the Cree, the musical *Kis-is-ski-tche-wan,* for "fast flowing."

Parkland, a verdant belt where the plains of the south meet the shield of the north. A well-treed, black-soiled strip of great fertility but incredibly short growing season.

Wildrose: Evocative of the freedom Meg longed for. A haunting promise of beauty and of fragrance.

And the Ferguson man, first name unknown, was looking for a wife.

The preacher continued his warning against bicycle hooliganism; Marlys's foot, in her button shoe of Vici kid with its fancy heel foxing and guaranteed to be the best shoe ever offered for its price ($1.25 from the small legacy each girl had inherited from their long-dead parents), stopped its swinging and began an impatient but soundless tapping. Wilda moved Daisy's drooping head to her lap.

And across the aisle the silvery-eyed Ferguson man from a place with the fetching name of Wildrose fixed his gaze on the speaker, but his thoughts were on . . . what?

Meg leaned back, turned her unseeing gaze upward and stared thoughtfully at the ceiling.

2

"I declare," Miss P's seatmate groaned, "this train is worse than the boat . . . I thought nothing could equal that!"

Miss P turned a sympathetic eye on the middle-aged woman mopping at her perspiring face and succeeding only in smearing the soot that flecked her weary countenance.

"And I do wish those boys would shut that window!" fretted the woman.

"It does serve to sweeten the air a little—," Miss P began mildly, only to be interrupted.

"Trains in England are much more civilized!"

"Well, so is the whole country, of course—"

"If I'd known this was such a . . . a *primitive* place, I'd never have agreed to come, sister or no sister!"

"Just how far are you going?" Miss P asked.

"Prince Albert. Named, I suppose, for our gracious queen's dear departed husband. But it can't be a compliment!"

"You can't judge the entire northwest by its trains," Miss P defended her chosen home. "Why, when we came—my father and mother and I—there *were* no trains."

"Don't tell me you came by prairie schooner!"

"My father did, bringing our things, locating his homestead, and getting it partially cleared and so on before he sent for us. Mother and I came by stagecoach. And I can tell you, it jounced ever so much more than this."

A particularly violent jerk sent the two women almost into each other's arms.

Straightening her hat and regaining her composure, Miss P forestalled any further shrieks on the part of her companion by saying, "We may as well get acquainted. We have the rest of the day together. I'm Phoebe Partridge. *Miss* Phoebe Partridge."

"Happy to meet you, I'm sure," the English lady said with dignity through her smut-stained smile. "I'm Edna Fishburn. Mrs. Edna Fishburn."

"And you are going to Prince Albert to meet your—"

"My sister. Her husband is ill, you see, and she needs help. They've been over here," and Mrs. Fishburn's vague wave took in the stretching prairies, not yet the green flowery meadows she had envisioned, but a dun-colored expanse stretching as far as the eye could see, "for years. Oooh! How has poor Esmie took it!"

"Well, really, Mrs. Fishburn, it isn't a bit like this where your sister is. This is prairie; Prince Albert is in bush."

"Tell me it's better . . . it couldn't be much worse." Poor Mrs. Fishburn's mug of tea, which she had been holding since she had plopped into the seat beside Miss P, slopped but, being half-cold, did no damage beyond another stain on that lady's travel-worn dress.

"It's much better," Miss P said, mopping at the damp spot on her new acquaintance's skirt with her handkerchief. "It's in the heart of the parkland and quite a flourishing little city. We manage to get in at least once a year for supplies. Usually, you see, we do our trading and buying at our local hamlet. Meridian, it's called."

"Meridian—is that where you live?"

"No, I live seven miles from there, in a district called Wildrose."

"Wildrose—I hope it's as lovely as it sounds."

"It's lovely," Miss P said firmly, adding thoughtfully, "a few months of the year, that is."

Mrs. Fishburn's eyebrows raised questioningly.

"Of course there is great beauty in snow too—," Miss P offered, not quite so positively. "There's just so much of it, you see, and it lasts so many months—" Miss P was definitely not as enthusiastic about life in Wildrose now.

"Winter," Mrs. Fishburn said, recalling England, "is a time for cozy fires, families drinking tea together, reading to your grandchildren . . ."

Mrs. Fishburn's reminiscences were interrupted by Miss P's sigh. A small sigh, but it was accompanied by a wistful expression that seemed to quite touch the heart of her new acquaintance.

The conversation lagged as Mrs. Fishburn remembered the introduction and the pronounced *Miss*. "Of course, one can enjoy tea with one's parents . . . and read around the fire . . ."

Mrs. Fishburn's alarm deepened when her companion sighed again. A deeper sigh.

Beginning to think she had blundered badly, Mrs. Fishburn hastened to change the subject. "And where have you been, Miss Partridge?"

"Just to Winnipeg," Miss P said, and the pensiveness faded from her middle-aged face. "I hadn't been back there since we left, over 30 years ago."

"My gracious! You really were pioneers, weren't you?"

"Indeed we were. We were among the first in our district. It's been something to see it grow—newcomers are still dribbling in from time to time, especially now that the economy is looking up. Why, there's a newcomer just a mile down the road from me—his family hasn't joined him yet either. I haven't seemed to be able to get acquainted with him."

And Miss P—as Mrs. Fishburn decided to retreat to the tiny, crowded "kitchen" that had been set up for the convenience of travelers—frowned and thought seriously of this newcomer to Wildrose, his need, and his independence. As committed as she was to the Golden Rule, "There has to be a way," she mused now. Perhaps if she could get him to attend her Sunday School class, it would break down his barriers. Neighbors, in the Territories, were often desperately needed by each other, and church, held in the schoolhouse, was one of the greatest bonds as it brought lonely people together. Miss P, teacher of the adult class, taught a positive gospel and, as much as was possible, lived it.

Now, however, another sigh escaped her.

Miss P had felt in her bones that her trip to Winnipeg would leave her counting—not her blessings, as she should have in light of the fact that Uncle Roscoe had willed all his earthly goods to her—but her grievances.

All unbeknownst to her, another sigh escaped her, a massive sigh.

Miss P didn't realize the sigh could be heard above the clatter of the train on the uneven tracks, the squall of weary babies and wearier mothers, and the shouts of children trying to entertain themselves in the narrow aisles.

But Mrs. Fishburn had returned to her place beside her new friend and heard, for the third time at least, a worrisome sound.

"Miss Partridge," she said, hesitantly, balancing the tea once again steaming enticingly, "are you all right?"

Miss P, chagrined at being caught in her gloomy thoughts, responded quickly. "Of course!"

Doubt replaced anxiety on the face of Mrs. Fishburn. Miss P, prodded by the look into a further assurance of her "all rightness," explained, "I've just come from a visit to my uncle's lawyer. To get his estate settled—that was the main reason for my trip out."

"Ah," nodded Mrs. Fishburn, sipping gently, "and he had just . . . just passed away."

"No, not really," Miss P continued. "It's been months. And I hardly knew him. It's been years, you see, since I saw him. But I was his only living relative. I was able," Miss P's explanation of her trip "out" faltered, "able to visit with old friends and girlhood chums."

"That must have been nice," Mrs. Fishburn said hopefully.

Miss P, recalling the reunion, sighed more deeply than before.

"You're doing it again," said her neighbor apologetically.

"I beg your pardon?" said Miss P, coming out of her obviously gloomy repinings. "Doing what?"

"Sighing."

Miss P bit her lip and turned her gaze to the flatlands flashing past the window of the train. At least they appeared to be flashing past—20 miles an hour, to her, was enough to make her dizzy. Never mind that one man had tossed his hat from the window, jumped off, claimed it, and made it back aboard without any trouble, to the huzzahs of onlookers equally as bored with the endless journey.

I never should have gone, Miss P thought for the hundredth time. *I knew how it would be.* And her faded eyes saw again the half-dozen friends with whom she had renewed acquaintance, and she shrank again from the conversations that had swirled around, everyone telling of their lives since they had last met.

Having finished her business about Uncle Roscoe's estate, pocketed a good deal of money and banked more, talked to the new owner of Roscoe's Implements, and agreed to a certain monthly amount to be mailed to her for the next dozen years, she had turned her attention to Monamae and Hazel and the others. Most of them, like her, were single now, but by death. But all of them—*all* of them—had family somewhere.

All but Phoebe Partridge.

Now, thinking about her paltry relationships, Miss P barely restrained another sigh. The afflicted Job, subject of a recent series of Sunday School lessons, had been a sigher. A sigher and a roarer, according to Scripture. That she resembled him in some small way gave Miss P a fleeting sense of satisfaction, a sign of the depths to which she had surely sunk.

"It must have been great fun," prompted a puzzled Mrs. Fishburn. "The reunion with old friends, I mean."

Fun? Fun, when the others reported their achievements while she had nursed her parents—first her mother, then her father—until their deaths? Fun, when she had carried on alone? Fun, when the others told of their visits to children and grandchildren and she had been stuck in the isolation of the backwoods? Fun, when they pulled out their albums and proudly displayed their offspring and their offspring's offspring? Fun, when she alone was totally without kith or kin or chick or lamb?

For the moment the loveliness of Wildrose, earlier spoken of to her seatmate, was buried under the loneliness of it. The coziness and comfort of her own fireside, so often thanked God for, took on a dark side only hinted at previously, and that in her darkest hours. For Miss P's ebullient spirit had made her an overcomer in all ways, and her Golden Rule had kept her busily and happily engaged in good works that had used up all of her spare time and more.

"I know exactly what it will be like," Miss P had predicted to Grandma Dunphy (not her own grandmother, of course; it was just another honorary title, like "aunt," which was given with respect to close acquaintances). "They'll all talk about their families. And me without even a cousin once or twice removed!" And she had brushed Grandma Dunphy's thin hair, as she so often did when she could get over to the Dunphy homestead, to add a little cheer to the old lady who lived with her son and his wife and six children, all busy making a living.

Grandma Dunphy, deaf as a post, had nodded agreeably.

"They'll all feel sorry for me," Miss P had lamented to Gerald Victor, her pastor, as she had come to church early as she always did, setting out a bouquet of chokecherry blossoms and searching out the box of crayons for the children's class.

And Pastor Victor, deep in a selection of hymns for the morning's service, had urged her to look up his old friend and pastor of that faraway congregation and had been no help at all. No one could be sorry for Miss P, his gentle smile had intimated.

But they had.

Bertha, once Phoebe Partridge's best friend, but whose letters had slowed and then ceased altogether more than 20 years ago, had shaken her gray head with an "Oh my, how sad," when Miss P had admitted that she had no living relatives now that Uncle Roscoe (whom she had never really known) had died. Then Bertha went on to enumerate her own quiverful of descendants.

And Florence Overton had stopped midsentence in her rave reviews of the Great Lakes visited on her honeymoon years ago, when Miss P confessed she had never been more than 20 miles from Wildrose in that many years and more.

Even her roomy handbag, crocheted for her by Sarah Tucker in appreciation for all Miss P had done for her household when Sarah was laid up with milk leg, was just another proof of the poverty of her life when compared to the handsome grained goat leather pocketbook proudly displayed by Hazel Crakes, sent by her son during his tour of the Mediterranean and featuring "a regular card pocket, besides one with flap and tuck, a coin pocket with polished snap frame, and two regular pockets." And from one of these Hazel had produced and cooed over the picture of that ever-so-successful son.

Miss P blew her nose with the hankie Anna Snodgrass had hand hemmed and given to her as a token of appreciation for the help she had been at Marta Szarvas's last lying-in. The same hankie Miss P had so willingly stained with tea when she had wiped the spill from Mrs. Fishburn's dress, perhaps ruining it forever, since the stain could hardly be washed out readily in the train's washbowl from which water slopped as quickly as it was put in because of the train's gyrations.

Mrs. Fishburn, looking anxious again, remarked now, "It must have been a—moving experience. The meeting with old friends, I mean," and patted Miss P's scrawny arm comfortingly. And when Miss P managed a watery smile, Mrs. Fishburn added, "You'll feel better, I'm sure, when you're in the bosom of your family again."

"I'm all alone," Miss P quavered. "All alone."

Mrs. Fishburn seemed unable to grasp such a state of affairs. "No brothers . . . no sisters . . . no children?" she breathed. "Not a nephew or a niece or . . . anyone?"

"I guess it's to be expected," Miss P said bravely, "when you live as long as I have and never marry."

"Oh my, how—," faltered Mrs. Fishburn.

"Sad," supplied Miss P.

And indeed, at the moment it did seem so. With a flicker of her ordinarily triumphant spirit Miss P realized that she hadn't been all that unhappy with her lot in life—until the reunion with old friends. But Mrs. Fishburn's expression was sympathetic, and Miss P weakly wallowed ever more deeply in the slough of despond. Or, she reflected, like Job, an ash heap.

Needing another hankie, Miss P fumbled with the one pinned to the bosom of her waist by a brooch made from the soft hair of little "Hanky" Chapman and made by his appreciative mother, Gussie, when Miss P had helped nurse her small son through a bad spell of croup.

Mrs. Fishburn, apparently deeply moved by her new friend's barren relationships, patted Miss P's arm again.

"But surely," she said, "surely there's *someone*. Someone has to meet you . . . seven miles from the Meridian station, you say?"

"Oh," Miss P managed, "Luther Boggs will be there."

"Luther Boggs? A . . . a *suitor*, perhaps?"

"Suitor! I left all that behind when . . ." and Miss P, staunching her tears, relayed how the one true love of her life had died years ago.

"No, Luther Boggs is the man who does my farming for me," Miss P explained. "He's half Indian, and I'm blessed to have him." Miss P, in spite of her sad outlook, admitted to at least one small blessing. "Luther and his wife live on my place in a shack of their own—"

"Shack! Oh my!"

"It isn't as bad as it sounds." Miss P dried her tears momentarily to defend her hired man's housing. "We call a small—er, domicile a shack. Really, I suppose, you'd call it a cabin. We use logs for everything, you know, or lumber."

And both ladies cast disparaging glances at the passing prairie in remembrance of scattered sod "domiciles" they had passed during the day.

"Yes, Luther will be there—" Unmentioned were the fire Luther would have laid in her range, the fresh milk and eggs in her pantry, the fresh bread baked by Lily, Luther's wife, the lamp cleaned and trimmed . . .

"Oh my," whispered Mrs. Fishburn. "Not a single kinsman!" It seemed the English lady was positively aghast at the thought.

"Not a kith or a kin," Miss P confirmed dolefully.

The hours flew by in melancholy consideration of Miss P's barren family tree. Even their shared lunch—a sandwich, a couple of boiled eggs, and an apple, along with more of Mrs. Fishburn's tea—was damped by sighs and sorrowful clucks by Mrs. Fishburn until interrupted by the call, "Next stop Meridian!"

"Oh here you are!" Mrs. Fishburn cried, sorting out their mutual wrappings. "I do trust, Miss Partridge, we may have opportunity to see each other again. Prince Albert, after all, is only 20 miles . . . you say you do get in there once in awhile . . ."

Miss P was reaching for her small case and the paper sack containing the snip snap (or slingshot) she was bringing young Buddy Victor, promised on his assurance that he would never use it on animals, birds, or persons; a taxidermist's manual she had found for Billy Szarvas; the *Everyday Cook Book and Cyclopedia of Practical Recipes* for new bride Meredith Gray; Aesop's Fables . . .

Miss P, struggling with her purchases, had no time to peer out the train window.

But a curious Mrs. Fishburn was doing so. "What's

going on?" she said with a note of surprise that the small hamlet's station platform should be so crowded. "You'll never find . . . what's his name? Luther—in that mob."

Straightening her hat and pinning it securely, Miss P prepared to disembark.

"I don't understand it," Mrs. Fishburn said plaintively. "I do wish you'd look—there's some kind of sign there. Could there be a celebrity on board?"

"Celebrity? For Meridian?" sniffed Miss P. But curious now, she bent her head and peered through the smoky window.

"Why," she said with surprise, "there's Brother Victor!" Looking more closely, she exclaimed, "And Sister Hubbard . . . and there's Dolly . . . and there's Gussie and baby Hanky—"

"Look at the banners," interrupted Mrs. Fishburn. "They seem to be welcoming someone by the name of Miss P. Does that make sense to you?"

But Miss P wasn't listening. "And there's Brother Tom and why, there's Grandma Dunphy—"

"But Miss Partridge," Mrs. Fishburn broke in to say, and who could blame her if she sounded slightly peevish, "I thought you said you didn't have any relatives!"

"So I did!" And Miss P nodded her head until the feather bounced on her best hat. "But I didn't say I haven't got any loved ones!"

A bewildered Mrs. Fishburn, watching Miss P turn toward the aisle, thought she heard her new acquaintance murmur fervently, "The Lord blessed the latter end of Job more than the beginning."

And Miss P stepped off the train into the arms of her church family.

3

With the singing of the Doxology and the prayer of benediction, Meg's attention settled, with a jolt, back to present circumstances. Danny was crowding past to get to the door and the outside quickly, and little Daisy was attempting to follow him, with Wilda hovering closely behind.

Meg stood in place as the congregation surged past. From across the aisle the Ferguson family prepared to join the stream, Mrs. Ferguson proudly and possessively holding her son's arm and introducing him to anyone who had come to the church since the "boys" had emigrated to the Northwest Territory.

"My son Royce," the matronly lady repeated, and the young man, probably nearing 30 (and certainly of an age to be seriously considering a wife!), bowed politely over hands proffered to him and flashed a smile that revealed teeth white against what was obviously an outdoorsman's face. This was no city man, Meg observed without any particular perspicuity on her part, and her interest sharpened.

Perhaps his enterprise on the homestead was paying off, or perhaps his doting parents had hurried him to the clothing store, but Royce Ferguson was very properly dressed in the shorter jacket, worn with lean pressed trousers, which had replaced the long frock coats of a few years ago. His face, besides being healthily colored, was squarish with a good strong mouth, equally strong nose, and those silvery eyes set under straight black brows and looking good-naturedly—now at least—at the world.

Clearly he already knew that beards and even moustaches were dated, for his clean-shaven face was tanned even where the black shadow indicated vigorous growth of hair, further evidenced by his close-cropped head, also "in fashion." Meg cast a glance at Harley and hoped he noticed the visitor's correct appearance and would do likewise. But Harley was blissfully unaware, his mouth and part of his chin hidden under a vigorous sprouting of hair and his sideburns flourishing magnificently.

Meg turned her attention back to the Ferguson family, now stepping into the aisle, and decided: *Whether conservatively and properly dressed or wearing blue denim, this is a man to look at twice. All the better!*

Marlys, just behind Meg, was impatiently muttering, "Move, slowpoke!" And to hasten her command, poked Meg with a sharp finger.

It was all the encouragement Meg needed. She stepped out, at the precise moment Mrs. Ferguson and her son turned their steps toward the door, followed closely by Becky, two younger sisters, and Roland Ferguson, father of this tribe.

How natural it was to meet the young man's gaze with a friendly, open smile. How simple it was to extend a gloved hand in response to Mrs. Ferguson's, "And this, Royce, is Meg Ferguson, recently come over from England. I believe you knew her brother and his family before you left . . . or did they come later . . ."

Mrs. Ferguson was lost, momentarily, in the toils of her introduction. It seemed perfectly natural for the man and

31

the girl to wait, smiling at each other, holding hands, mouthing a few stereotyped words, until with, "Well, it doesn't really matter!" Mrs. Ferguson moved on with her son, Meg naturally falling into step as they proceeded down the aisle.

Through additional introductions, numerous polite conversations, and a few warmer greetings from old friends, Meg was well content to walk casually with the Ferguson family past the threshold and the pastor's handshake to the steps and down to the street.

Becky, bright-eyed and proud of her handsome brother, closed in on Meg's other side with a droll but significant wink, as if to say, "What did I tell you!"

Before Meg had a chance to respond, she was jabbed again in the back. Marlys, unused to playing second fiddle, hissed in her sister's ear, "Move!"

Meg, usually compliant where Marlys was concerned—either because it didn't matter or to avoid confrontation—bore the insistent finger and command and stood her ground. There was, after all, something at stake here, and Meg was prepared to see it through even if it meant defying her stronger-willed sister.

"Royce," Becky was saying, drawing Meg forward, "Meg is my friend. Like me, she's fascinated with the idea of homesteading . . . learning about the West . . ."

Meg couldn't have said it better herself. She listened, silently applauding Becky's astuteness and basking in the smile Royce Ferguson turned on the two young women.

"Is that so?" he said. "We'll have to see to it that you both get your questions answered."

"Will you be staying long, Mr. Ferguson?" Meg asked.

"About two weeks," Royce Ferguson answered, and Meg decided, *That's enough time, for anyone as determined as I am!*

With Marlys virtually treading on her heels, Meg, rather naturally as it turned out, stepped down the street with Royce Ferguson, Becky on his farther side, heading home. It was only a matter of a few blocks, but for one as dedicated as Meg it was sufficient, she figured, for a first contact.

All those times she had seen Marlys play the game paid off now. Those very shenanigans she had despised in her sister, she now turned to her own advantage. Those subtle and not so subtle wiles would work for her as well as for her older, more experienced sister. After all, had she not learned from the master?

At another time, Meg would have blushed to see herself—face turned upward with fascination for the least word that fell from Royce Ferguson's lips; a bright laugh when his comment was the least bit scintillating. Hardest of all was the walk—it was all in the sway of the hips, the lift of the shoulders, the head held at what Meg assumed was a roguish angle, the eyelids lowered appropriately, the gaze direct at the proper moment.

Why, Meg thought, swaying until her skirt with its five-yard sweep swung like a bell around her slim ankles, it's all very simple.

And it seemed to work! Royce Ferguson had no trouble being talkative about what was obviously close to his heart: A place called Wildrose in the heart of the bush. And, at times, Meg had trouble remembering to play her role, being fully caught up in the fascinating subject.

True, her opening gambit was contrived, but after that it was easy: "What, Mr. Ferguson, is the difference between a buckboard and a buggy?"

"You know," the personable man said, "I've often asked myself that very question. They each have four wheels—except in England, of course, where they are a light, two-wheeled vehicle without a hood. They each can be pulled by one horse or two. Perhaps the difference lies in the spring system; the buggy traditionally has springs, the buckboard has a sort of springy platform; that is, the seat is mounted on an elastic board instead of springs."

Meg had no trouble appreciating the well-spoken explanation. So interested was she, in fact, that she forgot to bat her eyes as she had planned to do.

"We just call most such conveyances buggies," Royce said with a smile. "And most of them, in my neck of the woods, are pretty battered."

"Neck of the woods—what an excellent phraseology . . . for the bush country!" Meg said with just the right amount of light repartee in her tone.

Royce Ferguson laughed spontaneously and seemed to look at her with new interest.

"Of course," Meg continued, "we're well acquainted with buggies [they were passing all the time] and carts and even wagons; we use them, of course. But it truly seems they were made for the wide open spaces, don't you think? Soon, I guess, the motor car will become popular. What did you make of all those bicycles, Mr. Ferguson?"

"They were certainly distracting."

Meg had an idea Mr. Ferguson might have also had a moment's thought for the other distraction of the morning—Marlys's innocent (but oh so purposeful) display of ruffles and stocking. She gave a quick look back, where Marlys was walking rather stiffly, for Marlys, with Harley and Wilda and the children. Before she turned back, Meg caught a slumbering look from her sister's blue eyes, enough to say, "Look out, Missy!"

"Tell me, Mr. Ferguson," she said quickly, "how do you

34

feel about women being unable to file for a free homestead?"

"It'll come," Royce Ferguson said seriously. "But if
you're interested," he added with a smile, "you're much too
young to be considered."

"Why, Mr. Ferguson, thank you for the compliment! I'm
much older than I look. Does 18 seem young to you?" Meg
knew she was dissembling without really telling an untruth.
The truth was that 18 was still three months away.

"Eighteen! You don't say!" Royce Ferguson said, and
again it seemed he looked at Meg with new interest.

Becky took this moment to burst in pleadingly, "Royce—
let me go back with you! Why," she said, stumbling in her
earnestness, "I could be a big help to you and Neal! I can
cook and sew and keep house as well as Mother can!"

"Why, little sister," Royce said with surprise, "I believe
you're serious."

"I am! I am! I've given a lot of thought to it!"

"You could be mighty lonely," Royce said, "although
Wildrose is better settled than some areas, and houses are
not unreasonably far apart. Neal and I," he said thoughtfully, "could do with some female companionship. Available women, on the prairies or in the bush, are quickly
snatched up. You're too young to have any such ideas,
Becky." And Royce frowned at his little sister.

"Of course! I want to be with you and Neal. And I
love—I just love the bush!"

"Is it possible to 'just love' something you've never seen,
Miss Shaw?" Royce appealed to Meg.

"Oh, I quite agree with Becky. There are personalities, I
think, that are disposed to certain inclinations . . . that is,
they have a propensity for a particular way of life that might
be quite foreign to someone else." There, Meg thought with

35

satisfaction, that should sound adult enough to please him.

And sure enough, Royce was looking at her again with a special if somewhat surprised look on his face.

They stopped at the gate to the Shaw home. Royce opened it, looked down at Meg, and said thoughtfully, "Becky and I are going to take a walk this afternoon. May we have the pleasure of your company, Miss Shaw? We could, if you wish, talk some more about my homestead and life in general in the bush country."

"I'd love that above anything," Meg said and had no trouble sounding sincere.

"We'll stop by about two o'clock, then," Royce Ferguson said and tipped his derby.

This game of Marlys's, Meg thought half dazedly as she went up the walk to the front door, *has its uses after all.*

Marlys, coming hard on her heels, said sharply, "What kind of game, in heaven's name, do you think you're playing!"

4

"You really should act your age, Meg," Marlys said severely as the sisters, in their bedroom, changed clothes before helping Wilda get dinner on the table. "After all, you're only 17, you know."

"Why, Marlys," Meg said with honest surprise, "for years you've been telling me to act my age, and you always meant for me to act more grown up. Now you're advising me to act *young?*"

"You *are* young. This Ferguson man is no boy . . . he must be all of 10 years older than you. If you're going to flirt, do it with boys your own age."

"I'm not *too* young," Meg said quietly.

And she was right. The vast majority of girls were married early, some as young as 15. In fact, Meg thought briefly but was too kind to say, Marlys, in some people's thinking, might already be considered dangerously close to being an old maid.

But Marlys had had her chances, and they began when she was no older than the younger sister she now criticized. With her slim figure—which she early learned how to handle for the maximum effect—her blue eyes, ripe lips that pouted as easily as they smiled, and her piled masses of fair hair, young men, like bees to honey, had swarmed around.

Great-aunt Olivia had fretted and worried, but Marlys laughed and went her own way of pursuit and conquest. Great-aunt Olivia, Meg was sure, was relieved when at last Harley had written to say he was financially able to care for his sisters, with a sensible wife to oversee the young women. Marlys had cruelly and thoughtlessly left broken hearts behind.

Wilda did her best to make "ladies" of them. Here, as in England, Victorianism was strong. At 29, Wilda was already matronly, with great pride in her two-story brick house with its weather vane, gables, gingerbread trim, and veranda. She worked hard to maintain it, and their lifestyle, in the proper manner, dreaming of the day when she might employ more help than the childish, thin, half-starved Fanny, who came part-time.

Wilda's kitchen, though small and dark, was more convenient than the old-fashioned basement kitchens that many homes still had; it was fitted out with a good supply of crockery, pots and pans, and numerous new gadgets as they came on the market. However, Wilda scorned personal adornment, such as the "Puff Bang" ("Ladies who require a front piece will find this a little gem, light and fluffy, with a ventilated foundation"). Wilda would have benefited from such a hairpiece, rather than an escalloped silver and china centerpiece, in Meg's opinion.

Though Wilda's beauty aids were practically nonexistent, her kitchen bulged with helpful and even amazing aids to housekeeping. Small Fanny was all but overwhelmed by mincing knives, floor scrapers, raisin seeders, ice pick, tongs, chippers and shredders, a revolving slicer, meat chopper, and a fruit press. Meg sometimes thought, when Wilda introduced another of her modern conveniences, that it would have been better to give poor Fanny a few extra coppers a day as she struggled with the many "conveniences," which seemed to cause her more work rather than less.

As forward as she was in household acquisitions, Wilda was backward in accepting the idea of the "new woman." Meg and Marlys followed the fascinatingly reported efforts of Adelaide Hoodless, who would not settle for "God's will" as the reason behind the death of one child out of every five. Mrs. Hoodless objected strenuously and vocally to the flies that swarmed the milk that was delivered to the city, to children's long working hours, to the poor nutrition that helped fill graveyards with little tombstones. They applauded her every effort toward better nutrition and improved hygiene and bought, with their own money, her "little red book" with its calorie chart and guide to a healthy diet.

Wilda, with Fanny's help, was even now setting the table properly and serving up a meal heavy with potatoes, gravy, Yorkshire pudding, and roast beef, to be topped off with great rich slabs of apple pie (the apples duly prepared by Fanny on the new slicer).

Now Wilda's call came ringing up the stairwell: "Hurry on down, girls. I could use your help with the children."

About to pull an ancient dress over her head, Marlys paused, noting the "second-best" gown that Meg was hastily buttoning and patting into place. With a thoughtful look, Marlys put back the somewhat faded dress and chose, instead, the pale green Delineator with its long, slim, tight-fitting sleeve—definitely a move away from the balloon sleeves of '96. Thank goodness the bustle was finally gone! The new dress, while featuring the wasp waist (for the laced corset, of course, remained) was tight at the hips and flared beautifully into a bell shape. It was fresh and smart and, she knew, infinitely more flattering than Meg's blue percale, even with its epaulets trimmed with braid, collar and shoulder flaps ruffled, and its fancy flaring cuffs. Marlys envied the color; blue went so well with her own blue eyes and did very little, in her estimation, for Meg's hazel eyes.

Meg noticed Marlys's choice, and her eyes widened, then narrowed thoughtfully. The first glimmer of despair threatened, which Meg quickly cast off. Surely Marlys would have the grace to refrain from her experimentations since this was her own sister's first male friend. That Marlys suspected the afternoon outing, Meg was suddenly quite certain.

Meg knew the challenge a single man was to Marlys. To conquer, bring the man of the moment into a state of soft-eyed, rapt attention, and even to a passionate avowal of affection was everything to Marlys. Having reached this place, Marlys's interest quickly faded, her sweetness turned to scorn, her kindness to brittle disinterest. And many a young man had turned away, bewildered, and much wiser to the ways of women. *Some women,* Meg thought now, pinning up her hair and strengthening her determination to be all that a homesteader might need and want while being honest and sincere at the same time.

Dinner proceeded according to the Sunday schedule, the heavy food properly served by a scuttling Fanny; Danny and Daisy being patiently taught that children, even those as young as their three and four years, should be seen and not heard, as was right and proper. Harley assessed the morning's sermon and the pros and cons of the bicycle and finally decided, to Wilda's relief, that he would ride the cars to work. The bicycle, he maintained, was the cause of the gaiety that was marking the '90s.

"Yes, and," Wilda pointed out, "it has undoubtedly hurt

the churches, loosened manners, and been a chief contributor to the rise of the 'new woman.' "

"That Ferguson son seems like a decent sort of feller," Harley said, spooning out another helping of Yorkshire pudding. "Think so, Meg?" he asked archly.

"The Fergusons are a fine family," Meg said quickly, relieved to have an opening to ask, "Would you have any objection to my taking a walk with him and Becky this afternoon?"

"No problem, I'm sure," Harley said, expansive with good food and already half asleep.

"Help Fanny clear the table, girls," Wilda said, gathering a heavy-eyed Daisy in her arms and rising, motioning Danny to follow.

When the kitchen was clean and Fanny had taken her weary little self homeward, Meg settled herself in the parlor, ostensibly reading *Elsie Dinsmore*. She hoped fervently that Wilda would approve such Sunday reading and looked forward to an additional 20 books or so in the series taking poor Elsie from childhood to her holiday at Roselands, her marriage to a man much older (see—such marriages do work out!), Elsie's children, her "Journey on Inland Waters," her visit to the World's Fair, her grandmother days, and on and on.

Marlys chose to stay in the parlor rather than retreating to the privacy of their bedroom for her perusal of *Wee Wifie* by Rosa N. Carey. Meg knew that, hidden between the sofa cushions, was *Lord Lynn's Choice*, neither of which Wilda was apt to approve.

Harley was back downstairs, and Marlys's book was stuffed away when the doorbell sounded. "When the button is pushed the bell rings," Harley had announced when he had installed the four-inch nickel plated bell with "real

41

bronze push button and plate." "I'm winding it now," he had said, suiting action to words, "and it won't need to be wound again for six months." Daily when Fanny swept the front steps she polished the bell. Daisy and Danny had been severely admonished against pushing it and running down the mechanism.

Wilda answered the summons and invited, properly, the man and his sister into the parlor to be introduced to Harley. At Harley's invitation Royce and Becky Ferguson were seated. Marlys shot pointed looks at her brother.

"Oh, er, ahem," Harley said obligingly, "perhaps you haven't met my sister Marlys."

Royce rose again to his feet and bowed over the hand Marlys presented to him.

"Mr. Ferguson," Marlys said with deep interest, "I understand you are among the noble land seekers who are so valiantly settling our untamed West."

"I wouldn't say it is all that noble," Royce Ferguson said modestly. "But it certainly is a challenge."

"And your brother—Neal, is it?—he didn't choose to come home at this time?"

"One of us had to stay. We have stock to care for and chickens—"

"Chickens! How wonderful!"

"Well, I never thought chickens were all that wonderful, Miss Shaw. Perhaps you have helped me see them in a new light."

Meg looked at the man sharply; surely he was joking. But the brown face was as usual, handsome, manly, and his tone was polite.

"Now horses," Royce said with enthusiasm, "I can get excited about. We've just obtained a blooded stallion from Matthew Hunter, a neighbor of ours. Do you ride?" The question was addressed to the breathless, starry-eyed Marlys who, with pink lips charmingly parted, was the picture of total absorption and eager expectation.

"No, I'm very sorry to say. How I would love to learn!" *And have you teach me* was the big-eyed, silent invitation. Good old Becky. Stirring impatiently, she said, "Hadn't we better get on our way?"

"Of course! By the way, Mr. Shaw," Royce said, turning his attention to Harley, "would you have any objection if Meg accompanied Becky and me to The Ward—I have a particular reason for going."

"The Ward," Harley said, frowning. "That's our city's worst slum, you know. Not very savory for anyone, let alone females."

"I know, sir," Royce explained, "but I don't think there's any reason to think it's dangerous, at least in the broad daylight. Let me explain—"

And Royce Ferguson introduced them, with a heart-touching account, to a Jacob Lamb, another settler in the Wildrose district.

"His homestead, I understand, was claimed by a relative who, at his death, willed it to Mr. Lamb. Jacob came West about two years ago and has been working the land, clearing the bush, and fixing up a place decent enough for his family. His family lives here in Toronto. In The Ward, in fact. It's my understanding they moved to a place there when Jacob left, in order to save enough money to join him.

"Jacob had a good crop and has entrusted me with a fair sum of money for his wife. It's his hope that soon, with what they've been able to save, they can take the train West. Jacob is a fine fellow . . . very decent. I'm sure his family must be also."

"In that case," Harley said agreeably, "it would be an act

of mercy to see the woman and give her news of her husband and hand over the money. I don't see any reason why Meg shouldn't go with you. You'll be home before dark, of course."

Her face flushed with pleasure and anticipation, Meg hurried to get her hat and gloves. It was while she was pinning her hat before the hall mirror that she heard the plaintive voice of Marlys. "Is there anything I can do, Mr. Ferguson? Surely another *woman* [Marlys emphasized the word] might sum up the situation there. The needs of the slums is one of my burning passions!"

"An excellent idea, I'm sure," Royce Ferguson said warmly. "Thank you for thinking of it. Perhaps there is more that can be done for Jacob Lamb's family. Come on along, and welcome."

Meg thrust the hat pin savagely into her scalp and never felt the pain as Marlys brushed past, locating her hat and leaning in front of her sister to put it on. And smiling . . . smiling . . . smiling . . .

5

When Miss P's alarm sounded Sunday morning, her first waking thought was of her Saturday verse. Her second was that she wasn't all that happy about it.

Every night—after she had closed the dampers and set the oatmeal to cook on the back of the stove and just before she blew out the lamp—Miss P checked the Scripture calendar for the day's verse.

The useful and pretty publication was mailed to Miss P each new year by her Winnipeg friend Monamae Byers and was a publication of Monamae's church—no doubt a money-raising scheme, Miss P thought disapprovingly while nevertheless finding it very useful indeed. Not only did the monthly picture brighten the whitewashed log walls of Miss P's little home, but the daily Scripture verse was usually a source of comfort and strength.

It was Miss P's habit, upon retiring, to check the calendar, read the verse several times, assimilating it as she drifted off to a good night's sleep, and repeating it if she woke in the night. It was a great alternative, she believed, to troubling thoughts that tended to crowd one's mind otherwise.

Ordinarily, on waking, Miss P was pleased to remember her verse. Not so with her Saturday verse.

Still filled with wonder at the reception her Wildrose

friends had given her on her return from Winnipeg, and basking in the warmth of their love (almost like a real family, she allowed herself to believe), she had come home to find—as she had anticipated—her home warm; her cupboards filled with milk, butter, and eggs; and a fresh loaf of bread exuding its fragrance from the warming oven.

Luther, having met her as expected, had brought her home, listening patiently to her report of her trip, and had driven off to the barn with the rig and horse. Lily, his wife, a middle-aged, comfortably cushioned, and smiling woman, had thrust her dark face in for a moment to welcome Miss P home.

Miss P had unpacked, put her white gloves to soak in the preparation of laundering them later for tomorrow's church service, scrambled two eggs, made a pot of tea and a piece of toast from Lily's bread, dipped water from the range's reservoir for her Saturday night bath, and—warm and clean and glowing with satisfaction—wound her clock and checked the day's verse.

Reading it, she was stricken. Instead of being the edifying experience she usually enjoyed, Miss P was rudely stung by the words.

And the Saturday verse had resulted in a restless night and disturbed her waking thoughts. Miss P was inclined to be annoyed with Mr. Able of Able's Funeral Home; it was too bad of him to include such a verse, she thought crossly now as she awoke to the ring of her alarm clock, threw back the covers, and stretched her bony feet toward her slippers.

Even getting busy with her morning responsibilities didn't help. The offending scripture, like a troublesome toothache, refused to be ignored.

"James 2:26" (Miss P was particular about memorizing the reference along with the verse.) "For as the body without the spirit is dead, so faith without works is dead also."

Miss P had always considered herself a woman of faith. Certainly faith had stood her in good stead when she had gone through those testing years of nursing her parents; even thinking of those days caused Miss P to pause in her biscuit making and raise a fervent note of thanksgiving for Luther and Lily Boggs and their appearance to take over the work of the homestead and to help in the house.

But all things considered, Miss P now, being the honest and scrupulous soul that she was, found her confidence shaken in her standing as a woman of faith. "Dead . . . dead . . . dead," the fateful words nibbled away at her peace of mind. "Faith . . . without works . . . is dead . . . dead . . . dead . . ."

She couldn't escape them as she took the light, golden biscuits from the oven, put six of them in a basket, covered them with a snowy towel, and opened the door on a beautiful bush spring day. The flashing birds and their outpourings of song, the fragrance wafting from the opening buds of the lilac at the corner of the house—none of these charmed her as they usually did.

Quickly Miss P walked across the yard to the small, tight "shack" or cabin of Luther and Lily Boggs.

"My usual Sunday morning offering," Miss P said with a smile, handing the basket to Lily.

"Oh, it's so good to have you home again!" Lily said and received the Sunday morning blessing with a smile creasing her shining brown face.

This ritual over, Miss P went into the second certainty of her Sunday morning. "I hope you and Luther will come to church today, Lily. I'd like particularly to have you in my Sunday School class."

And as usual, Lily's broad face dimmed. "We'll see,

47

Miss P," she murmured, as she always did. And with another warm smile Miss P turned back to her own home.

"Some day!" she encouraged herself as she returned to her breakfast.

But for once she could find no satisfaction in the small joys of her life—she poured boiling water into the old brown teapot and could not relish this treasure from her grandmother's ancient kitchen; she served her oatmeal in its blue bowl, stirring in golden cream and brown sugar, and completely overlooked her usual admiration of the rich mix of colors; she broke her biscuit and applied creamy butter and glowing pin cherry jelly and they were as colorless blobs, without the satisfaction of a task well done. The tasty food was as sawdust.

Miss P washed her few dishes, threw the sudsy water into the yard, and could find no amusement in the churning legs of the chickens as they surged toward it hopefully. Nor could she laugh at their optimistic but fruitless pecking of the multicolored bubbles.

The verse, she concluded with a sigh, could not be shrugged off, and she sadly acknowledged her lack of works. Of what good, she reasoned, was all her faith, if acceptable works did not follow?

For once Miss P could find no pleasure in her good navy blue dress with its neat white collar and buttons. She stepped blindly into her Sunday shoes, usually a source of satisfaction. Ordered from the catalog, of course, and almost the only pair not featuring the pointed "coin toe," the "98 cent Congress shoe, made from a good quality of serge, leather soles and counters, with a commonsense last and guaranteed cool and comfortable," had lost their appeal this day, and all because of the nagging scripture and its effect.

Miss P settled her plain black hat on her skimpy hair and

yanked off the small feather she had added to the narrow
brim (imitation hair and braid mixed), feeling it added a
jauntiness she had no right to claim. Her gloves had dried
overnight and she put them on, picked up her Bible, tucked
her offering into her purse, and failed to find her spirits
lifted by the extra funds she was able to add because of
Uncle Roscoe's legacy.

Luther had the buggy at the door and helped a doleful
Miss P up into it and handed her the reins.

"Thank you, Luther," Miss P said in such a funereal
tone that Luther went back to his shack shaking his head
and observing thoughtfully to Lily, "We may just have to go
to church one of these days."

The first homestead that Miss P encountered belonged
now to Jacob Lamb. New to the district, he was inclined to
keep to himself. Miss P, try as she might, had made no
headway in getting acquainted. Mr. Lamb was crossing his
yard, milk pail in his hand, and Miss P pulled to a stop, as
she often did on a Sunday morning, and called, "Mr.
Lamb—good morning!"

Jacob Lamb, without missing a step, tipped his work-
weary cap and continued.

With a sigh Miss P slapped the reins on the horse's back,
clucked in encouragement, and proceeded to the next property. Turning into the grassy yard, Miss P stopped at the
rude handmade door of a small cabin. She had no sooner
pulled to a halt than the door opened and a small girl
emerged.

"Good morning, Margie," Miss P said cordially and
reached a hand to help the child up into the buggy. Margie
settled herself happily beside her friend and chattered on
about her baby brother, her new kittens, her little garden . . .

Miss P remembered Margie's gift, brought from Manitoba, and pulled from her purse a handful of colorful ribbons, just made, she had thought, for Margie's vigorous, untamed head of hair.

"Oooh, Miss P!" Margie breathed, over and over again. "I just love 'em, specially this purple one!" Reluctantly she turned them over to Miss P to be kept until their return from Sunday School and church.

To her Sunday School class, the Worthy Warriors, Miss P projected her usual spirited, buoyant image but felt it all a farce. At the close of the class she hugged a lonely, discouraged young wife and whispered to Buddy Victor that she had not forgotten the snip snap he so badly wanted, then settled herself in her usual "pew"—a badly carved, ink-stained desk—and hoped for some encouragement for her battered spirit from the church service.

It was not to be. Even as the group lustily sang "We've a Story to Tell to the Nations," Miss P's heart was crying, "What, oh, what can I do for You, Lord?"

Past the prime of life, with limited strength, no talent, and the backwoods for a mission field, it seemed that the time and opportunity to "work" for the Lord had slipped away. It seemed confirmed by the next hymn selection. Miss P's voice quavered, dry as dust:

> *"Work, for the night is coming,*
> *Under the sunset skies:*
> *While their bright tints are glowing,*
> *Work, for the daylight flies.*
> *Work till the last beam fadeth,*
> *Fadeth to shine no more;*
> *Work, while the night is dark'ning,*
> *When man's work is o'er."*[*]

[*]Annie L. Coghill, "Work, for the Night Is Coming."

Miss P couldn't grieve as fully as she might have liked, since Charity Szarvas's baby was fussing. The little one, obviously teething, and fretful in its long dress of white cambric elaborately tucked and embroidered and feather-stitched (made by the child's loving Aunt Modesty, Miss P knew, when the expectant mother drooped, hopeless, her character stained and her future grim. Thank God! Miss P thought now, that this had been a story with a happy ending!). And thank God Charity and her strong, loving husband were in church.

And they needed what Pastor Victor's message could do for them. Miss P laid aside her Bible and purse and turned to the young embarrassed mother and, with a smile, held out her arms. With a relieved sigh Charity relinquished the baby, and Miss P slipped outside to walk the grasses of the school playground and hum "Rock-a-bye-baby" while the group inside sang "Rock of Ages."

When the morning service was over Miss P returned the baby to her mother, and friendly hand gripped friendly hand for the first time in at least a week. Miss P was surrounded by welcoming arms and warm greetings. But Miss P's ears seemed to hear, instead, the murmur of voices from far-off lands, calling "Come over into Macedonia and help us," and in place of the present outstretched hands she imagined black and brown and yellow hands were beckoning, beckoning uselessly and poignantly, for her to come. It was all too late, Miss P mourned.

When the buggy was trundling Miss P and Margie back down the bush-bounded road, past a few broken acres, small fields, and endless stretches of virgin growth, the child bounced until the spring seat heaved and tilted.

"Was Daniel in a real lions' den?" the small girl from the unchurched home asked. "And did a really truly angel shut their mouths? Or is that a fairy story?"

"It's true," Miss P said, as she did most Sundays, and went on to explain that Daniel's God also took care of small girls, and His angels watched over them.

"See you next week," Margie chirped when the buggy stopped at her door.

Miss P smiled and handed Margie her ribbons, but inside her spirits were very low. "Oh," she grieved, "if there was only something . . . something special . . . I could do."

After a meager noon meal, Miss P hunted out her rag bag and located a few scraps of surah silk. It was enough, she was sure, so that on Monday—the day of rest over—she could make Charity's baby a cool, loose-cut but dainty dress in which the wee mite would be comfortable.

On a sigh, the day came to an end. Miss P put her gloves to soak, measured out tomorrow morning's oatmeal, braided her graying hair, checked the dampers, donned her summer-weight nightgown, and picked up the clock.

Winding the clock, her eyes went automatically to the Scripture calendar and the Sunday verse. She read it once, twice, three times.

In the lamplight Miss P's wrinkled cheeks flushed and her faded eyes shone. And when she climbed into bed she knew—she just knew—she would have a restful night.

Miss P closed her eyes and recited her Sunday verse: "Mark 14:8—'She hath done what she could.' "

6

"Well, I guess we're off," Royce Ferguson said as Meg and Marlys entered the parlor, Marlys's eyes bright with anticipation, Meg's usually sunny face unusually flushed. No doubt Royce found her pink cheeks attractive, for he smiled down on her, and after he had herded the three girls off the veranda, down the walk, through the gate, and onto the sidewalk, he offered his arm to her, with another smile.

Although Becky had walked abreast with Royce and Meg on the way home from church, now, with Marlys along, she wisely stepped back and she and Marlys followed the neat broad back of Royce and the slim waist and swinging skirts of Meg.

Although the city's street-railway had converted to electric power a few years previously, walking, particularly on a Saturday or Sunday afternoon, was very popular, and the closer to the main thoroughfares they went, the more thronged the sidewalks became. Everyone, it seemed, was either heading for or coming from glittering King Street. On Queen Street, not quite so fashionable nor favored, Timothy Eaton had chosen to set up his remarkable store— cash only, but perfect satisfaction guaranteed. His catalog sewed down the West as surely as Red Fife Wheat.

"Now that," Royce said as they paused before the big

show window to study the amazing display of available merchandise, "is what we need in the bush," and he pointed to "The New Graphophone Talking Machine."

"Why, Royce?" asked Becky, peering at the poster alongside the 26-inch-long japanned tin amplifying horn and the open case of 24 tubular musical and talking records. "So you can make $5 to $25 an evening by giving public exhibitions?"

"Nothing like that," Royce said with a laugh. "No, I was thinking about hearing a voice—any voice—in the long silences of the longer northern winter evenings."

"But don't you and your brother live together?" asked Meg.

"Not really. You see, we chose homesteads side by side, and we each built our cabin almost on the line. True, some of the time we bunk up together, particularly if one of us has made a good gopher stew . . ." Royce was obviously teasing, and the girls obliged by grimacing and squealing.

"Maybe I don't want to go with you after all!" Becky said.

"The one really good reason I'd have for taking you," Royce said, "is to have someone help with the cooking. I get mighty tired of bannock, beans, and potatoes!"

"If you want company, Mr. Ferguson," Marlys said archly, "how about the magic lantern? This one, see, is cut away so you can see the kerosene lamp inside . . . isn't that, er, cute? And see," she said, squinting her blue eyes and reading, "slide number eight will give you unadulterated pleasure through: 'True Romance,' 'Come into the Garden, Maude,' 'If I Were to Tell You All I Feel,' and more."

"Pretty cold company, I'd say," Royce said with a laugh. "What we bachelors need is a wife. Not everyone, you know, is willing to take on the hard work, loneliness, and sacrifice that are demanded of pioneer women."

"I should think," Marlys said in tones that pulsated with fervency, "a woman would consider it a great honor to be invited to share such an enterprise."

"Do you indeed?" Royce sounded thoughtful. "I would have thought that you, Miss Shaw, were totally committed to a life of comfort, even luxury, here in the city. This is indeed an eye opener . . ."

"I've always said," Marlys breathed with a sincerity that made Meg's eyes widen in disbelief, "that it was worth any sacrifice to breathe the woodsy air, see the magnificent sunsets and star-studded nights, and, yes," Marlys seemed exalted and visionary, "know the thrill of seeing the black virgin soil turn to the sharp edge of the plow—"

"Well said, Miss Shaw!" Royce exclaimed. "Could it be that you have a poet's heart?"

Marlys lowered her eyes and, yes, *blushed. How can she blush on cue?* Meg wondered, admiring as well as despising the sham.

It seemed only natural, as they moved on from the store window, that Marlys should fall in step with Royce. "Call me Marlys, please," she was saying as Meg and Becky exchanged glances, Becky rolling her eyes, Meg shrugging her shoulders.

She had seen it so many times. Often they were callow youths, who all but fell over their feet in their eagerness for a smile from the fair Marlys. But more and more it had been men of sincere feelings, whose approaches had been met with seemingly equal sincerity—for a time. But always Marlys tired of the conquest and shed one vassal for another. Just now there was no one, and Meg could see that Marlys was enjoying the challenge of someone like Royce Ferguson—no longer a boy, decidedly attractive, and here for only a short time. But enough time, Meg thought despairingly, for Marlys to have the stimulation on which she thrived. And for me, Meg thought drearily, to lose my chance.

For Meg knew that eventually Marlys would lose her interest, and Royce, as the others before him, would be there if one cared to take Marlys's leftovers and pick up the pieces.

"I'd even do that!" Meg brooded.

Marlys's castoffs had never appealed to Meg. But Royce, whether first or secondhand, was a man worth having. And with him, Meg was honest enough to admit, came a homestead, the bush, and Wildrose! And Meg turned her back, finally and forever, on her ephemeral, unsubstantial, intangible dreams of the prairie.

"The city has certainly changed," Royce was saying, looking around at the riotous passing parade. "Before I left, wages had been cut and families suffered. The week's pay— for an 11-hour day, six days a week—was between $6.00 and $8.50. It made it easy to leave, that's for sure.

"Things don't seem to be much better even now, for the poor," Royce continued. "There are just as many boys on the street asking for pennies—"

"Well, Sunday is a good day for it," Becky interposed. "Lots of people are out on the streets, many of them with money in their pockets, all dressed up, in an expansive mood."

"Like us," Meg said, having already doled out a handful of coins to one raggedy, red-eyed, shriveled-appearing child of indeterminate age and undoubtedly poor health.

"Look at this," Royce said, stopping at the gate to a large, prepossessing looking house and pointing to a black mark on the fence post. "Do you know what this is?"

"Of course," his sister said promptly. "We see things like this all the time—it's the hobo's way of passing on a message to other hobos."

"Right. This small square shape, point down and with one side slightly open, means 'ferocious dog.' " And even as they paused, vicious snarls could be heard emanating from behind the closed door.

"A circle with a dot in the middle means 'good for nothing.' A sort of thick circle means 'have given and will probably give again.' Neal and I, though we didn't have any need to beg, thank God, went across the country with very little; what we had, we often shared with transients. My heart goes out to them—"

"Wait—look," Meg said quietly, putting out her hand and bringing the party to a halt. In front of them was a house, shuttered, blinds half drawn, and with a quart of milk on the stoop. Even as they watched, a stealthy movement in the front bushes materialized into a boyish figure. Furtively it crept up the steps, snatched up the bottle, and slipped around the side of the house and disappeared.

"Why, the little thief!" Marlys gasped. "The nerve! Oh, the depravity!" She looked around. "We must report it!"

"Report what?" Royce offered mildly. "One child, whose face we didn't see, skinny and underfed like they all are. Barefooted as they all are, wearing a hat as they all do. No doubt the evidence has disappeared into his hungry little tummy by now."

"A white duck sailor hat!" Marlys said triumphantly. "And with an identifiable colored braid on the band. *And*," she went on with relish, "he had *red hair!*"

"Well," said Royce mildly, moving on, "I'm not inclined to pursue the little beggar. It would mean the hoosegow for sure. How much help would that be?"

"Oh, Royce, you're so wise!" Marlys said now, blue eyes wet with ready tears and pink mouth tender. "Blessed are the merciful."

How can she cry tears on cue? Meg thought, dumbstruck again at her sister's performance.

Their steps had been taking them inexorably toward the more unsavory part of town. Soon it was as if they had stepped into another world. Homes, having grown successively more and more ramshackle and less and less presentable, changed to wretched tenements. Children played in the narrow streets and alleys, men lounged in doorways, women leaned for a breath of air from open windows from which clotheslines stretched and ragged garments drooped in the fetid air.

The girls, in spite of themselves, walked more closely to Royce, aware of looks that, if not cunning and manipulative, were sullen.

Checking an address on a paper he withdrew from his pocket, Royce turned into an open doorway and knocked on the first door he came to. It was opened by a hunched, middle-aged man, his black coat greasy, his shirt collar wrinkled. He stared at his callers suspiciously.

"Sir," Royce said politely, "do you know a Mrs. Amanda Lamb?"

Silence. The man sucked his teeth and narrowed his eyes.

"I have a message for Mrs. Lamb, at this address, from her husband."

"His name?" the nasal voice asked.

"Jacob Lamb. I'm a neighbor of his."

"From?"

"Saskatchewan. The post office is Meridian." Suddenly inspired, Royce pulled a battered envelope from his pocket and held it out for the man to see.

"Top floor, last door on the right," the man said and pointed to the dirty, carpetless stairs.

Royce thanked the man, who watched their progress from his doorway. Silently the four trooped up three flights of stairs to the top floor, turned down a hall on which broken linoleum cracked underfoot, and stopped at the proper door. Royce knocked.

The door opened a few inches.

"Yes?" The voice, soft and gentle, was indrawn, almost with a gasp, and seemed tense with fear.

"Mrs. Lamb?" Royce asked. "Mrs. Amanda Lamb?"

"Yes."

"May we come in, Mrs. Lamb—"

"Is it about Freddy?" The question was quick, anxious. "Is he in some kind of trouble?"

"Freddy? No, Mrs. Lamb, it's about Jacob. He asked me to come see you."

"Jacob! Is he—is Jacob all right?"

"Just fine, Mrs. Lamb. Perhaps I should explain that I'm a neighbor of his."

The door was flung open. "Oh!" the woman gasped. "Oh, you are so welcome!"

Royce and the three young women with him filed into the first room of what seemed to be a two-room apartment.

"Come, children!" the woman called, and five children, one carried by the oldest girl, came from the other room where it seemed they may have gone when the knock sounded on the door.

"It's someone from Papa, children! Isn't that good news! Find chairs for the guests, Jake. Ammie, put Kerry down and come meet Papa's neighbors."

Finding chairs in what was an extremely bare but extremely clean room, Royce introduced himself.

"And is one of you, by any chance," a smiling, thin-faced woman asked, "Miss P?"

The girls looked mystified, and Royce laughed. "No, but I can see your husband is quite a letter writer."

"Yes, he has introduced us quite fluently to all his new neighbors. In preparation, you see, for when we join him."

"Perhaps," Royce said cheerily, "it will be sooner than you had thought. I understand from Jacob that this envelope," and he put it in a worn, trembling hand, "contains funds for that purpose."

Mrs. Lamb glanced inside, clasped the envelope to her heart, and tears rose in the weary eyes and splattered down on the envelope and the faded dress.

"Don't, Mama, don't!" The oldest girl in the group knelt by her mother's side. "She hasn't cried, you see, all this time," the child said, turning to the company watching with sympathetic faces. "She can take all kinds of hard knocks, our Mum, but good news turns her all soft."

The tears were turning to smiles. "It seems, children," the mother said, "we may be able to go be with your father . . . we'll read his letter after our guests leave. Now, Mr.—"

"Ferguson, Ma'am." And Royce introduced his sister and Meg and Marlys.

"Tell us about Wildrose, Mr. Ferguson," Amanda Lamb begged. "It sounds . . . well, it sounds like heaven to us," and her glance took in the barren room, the poorly clad children, and the one pot simmering on the stove.

"But first," she said, "you must meet the children. Jacob will want to know all about them." Amanda Lamb's excitement showed in the two red spots that glowed on her white cheeks and in the fit of coughing that overtook her. Ammie put her arms around the frail figure and held her mother tightly until the paroxysm had passed.

Royce and Becky and Meg and Marlys looked at each other uneasily.

"This," the gasping voice spoke at last, "is Jake . . . named for his father, of course." Jake, about 16 or 17 years old, nodded politely. "Ammie, who is 13, is named for me.

"And these two, who look like twins but aren't," Mrs. Lamb said, "are Joe and Josephine." (Eight and nine seemed about right.) That left Kerry, the baby of the family, a toddler three years old, clinging like a limpet to Ammie's skirt.

"There's one more," the mother said, and a shadow seemed to pass over her thin face. "Freddy—Freddy should be home any minute—"

Even as she spoke the door opened and a boy slipped inside. A barefoot boy. A boy with red hair flaming beneath a white sailor cap. A cap with a distinctive colorful braid.

A boy with a bottle of milk under his arm.

"Oh, Freddy! Milk!" The mother spoke breathlessly, smothering a cough. "You blessed boy!

"Freddy is such a help," the woman said proudly to her startled guests. "We couldn't make it without the money he earns and the things he brings home, though we all—except Kerry, of course—do *something* to add to the funds we are saving to go be with Jacob. Wildrose—where it's healthy and clean. And," she finished simply, "where there'll be milk and to spare. Freddy—this is just what we need!"

"What *you* need, Mama." The boy Freddy looked with loving and anxious eyes at the white face turned on him so fondly as he set the bottle on the table. "I got it for you, Mama."

7

Miss P was troubled.

Committed as she was to the Golden Rule, there seemed no way she could "do unto others" where her new neighbor was concerned. Jacob Lamb resisted all overtures and offers of help, though in Miss P's viewpoint he was that most pathetic of all creatures—a bachelor.

It was a great challenge to Miss P.

Not that Miss P ever considered bachelorhood a state to be challenged. No indeed. Miss P was content with her lot as a spinster. True, at times her single estate didn't seem as "blessed" as popular opinion labeled it, but that was only during the lonely hours. Lonely hours when Luther and Lily were snug beside their own fire, the evening was long, and the house had no echo of another voice. Then, in desperation, Miss P was reduced to talking to Tom Bigbee, her cat.

The lonely little corner in Miss P's heart had been warmed and filled when her loving church family had gathered to greet her with open arms when she returned from Winnipeg. But only temporarily. Miss P had all the instincts of a broody hen in the springtime, and her empty nest disquieted her otherwise happy spirit on a regular basis.

At those times, as now, Miss P stirred up her nest,

making a great to-do with her cleaning and rearranging, baking and cooking. Now again, alone in her well-ordered home, cookies spreading their fragrance throughout, only the persistent sound of an unwelcome fly buzzing on the spotless window broke the silence.

It was simply not to be borne. Restlessly, Miss P had gone over her options. They were: take down the curtains and wash them or do something for someone else.

Always, when faced with such a choice, doing something for someone else won out.

But for whom? Charity Szarvas's baby had her new dress; Grandma Dunphy's hair had been attended to yesterday; the Sunday School papers had all been delivered to the absentees; she could think of no one sick or ailing.

Naturally, her thoughts turned to her neighbor, still as much a stranger to her as when he had moved in almost two years ago.

Jacob Lamb—working his old uncle's farm, and working hard, had little time for socializing—didn't even get to church. Maybe the man was a heathen. But Miss P didn't think so; he was just so everlastingly caught up in getting the old house in order (uncle had built hastily and was no example of what bachelorhood could be, at its best). Jacob Lamb had a family back east—Toronto, Miss P thought, and had sometimes delivered a letter to his door when she had been to Meridian to the post office and had collected mail for everyone along her route, as was the custom.

Just yesterday, returning from Grandma Dunphy's, she had met Jacob Lamb, coming toward her in his rig. Not only had Miss P pulled to the side of the bush-bounded road but had halted, a sure sign that she had something to say. Jacob Lamb should have, by rights, stopped his rig alongside, tipped his hat, smiled, and greeted her.

But Jacob Lamb, though he did tip his hat politely enough, had simply driven on. Now here were all these raisin-filled cookies, and no open door to receive them.

"I think, Tom Bigbee," Miss P said, "I'll have to go have a talk with Pastor Victor."

Suiting action to words (stopping only long enough to eliminate the invader on her windowpane), Miss P donned her hat and made her way to the barn. Luther being gone, she efficiently put the harness on Old Mag, hitched her to the buggy, climbed in, waved at Lily who had peered out of her window, and turned her rig toward the parsonage.

"Miss Partridge!" Ellie Victor called cheerily from an open door. "Get down and come on in." Which Miss P did as soon as she had tied Old Mag to the parsonage fence.

"Cup of tea?" Ellie asked affectionately. This was one church member, she knew, whose coming she didn't have to dread. Though burdened at times, she was never a burden; she might be troubled, but she was never a trouble-maker. Miss P righted more problems than she caused.

"Is Pastor in?" Miss P asked, almost first thing, and Ellie Victor smiled. Obviously Miss P had come for counsel. Calling her husband from his "study," Ellie Victor poured boiling water into a teapot, fetched her best cups and spoons, lifted dainty serviettes from the buffet drawer, and brought in a plate of just-sliced fruitcake.

"Miss P!" her pastor greeted her warmly, accepted a cup of the fragrant brew and a hefty slice of cake, and seated himself.

Miss P never beat around the bush (unless some devi-ousness was necessary for her plan), and she came straight to the point.

"You know, Brother Victor, how I'm committed to the Golden Rule."

"Doing unto others as you would have them do unto you."

"Right. But now here's Jacob Lamb—"

"Your neighbor."

"Right. And he won't let me *do unto him!*"

"Hm. He is a pretty independent fellow, all right. Even I haven't really gotten next to him. Seems consumed with the need to get his family out of the city and here on the homestead."

"Well, I'd like to help. There must be a great deal one could do to that house . . . hasn't been taken care of for years, not properly." And Miss P sniffed, thinking of the uncle and nephew—*bachelors*—who had kept house there. ("Keeping house"—it was as descriptive as "making land," the homesteader's term for clearing the bush.)

"I'm sure you've tried?" the pastor asked, knowing well this particular parishioner.

"Everything, short of thrusting my help upon him. You know, one day he'll need someone and need them very badly indeed . . . as we all have, and he won't feel free to ask, I'm afraid."

"It's rather . . . ticklish, you being a woman and him living alone."

"Pastor! As if anyone could accuse me of improper motives!" Miss P was scandalized.

"None of us who know you, dear friend."

Mollified, Miss P sipped her tea.

"Maybe it works in reverse," she said suddenly.

"It?"

"Doing unto others," Miss P said thoughtfully, almost immediately adding, "For a proud man, maybe it works in reverse." And leaving her pastor chewing on that and shaking his head, Miss P thanked Sister Victor for the tea and cake and took her departure.

Watching her gaunt upright form spin out of the yard, her hat rigidly straight on her thinning hair, her eyes alight behind her spectacles, Gerald Victor murmured, "Poor man—hasn't a chance. I hope he's ready for our Miss P."

8

"Your hat, Freddy," his mother said quietly.

Freddy quickly removed the white sailor hat with its incriminating braid. His red hair, wildly and luxuriantly curly, rioted over his forehead and into the watchful blue eyes now studying the strangers seated in his home.

Did he see us, Meg wondered, as we watched at the gate when he made his dash to the stoop with its milk free for the taking? Meg heard Marlys's indrawn breath and glanced at her quickly. Marlys, lips parted, seemed ready to expose the boy's act. Meg, watching Amanda Lamb's renewed and poorly stifled fit of coughing, the children's anxious concern for her, and Freddy's suddenly despairing glance in his mother's direction, spoke quickly.

"I think perhaps we should be going. Mrs. Lamb has her family's supper ready, and we need to get home before it's dark."

"You're right, of course," Royce Ferguson agreed and just as quickly.

Marlys, her face a study and her lips tightening, subsided.

"Why," Mrs. Lamb said, recovering her voice, "we haven't even offered our guests the courtesy of a cup of tea. Ammie, fill the teakettle—"

Ammie looked startled at the suggestion but turned slowly to obey.

Was there the luxury of tea in this pitiful abode, Meg wondered, and was relieved when Royce said firmly, but kindly, "Another time, Mrs. Lamb. I'm sure you have much to talk about with your children, and they will all want to hear their father's letter."

The eyes of all, under hair of variously tinted shades of the vibrant color that lit the tousled head of Freddy, turned eagerly toward the envelope still clasped to Amanda's bosom.

Rising, the woman followed them to the door, the children pressing silently behind her. Almost like a rear guard, Meg thought. Freddy alone stood back by the table with its incriminating bottle of milk, his eyes watchful.

"Will you come again?" the tired voice questioned. "I suppose you are returning to Wildrose soon?"

At Royce's nod of assent, she continued, "I could have an answer ready. I know it would be an imposition—"

"I'll be happy to take it," Royce assured her and was rewarded with a relieved smile.

Mrs. Lamb's final farewell was interrupted by another painful series of racking coughs. Royce, Becky, Meg, and Marlys stopped uncertainly in the doorway until Jake, with the awkward grace of the half-boy, half-man that he was, said, "Come, Mama, you've gotten too excited."

"But it's been so good!" Amanda managed, meanwhile allowing her son to turn her back, shutting the door with a final nod and an assurance that his mother would be better "tomorrow."

Silently the group made its way down the hall, the stairs, and past the half-open door and watching man within. Royce nodded in the general direction of the landlord and the door that bore the indistinct sign "Lev Rosen."

The door opened, and the man stepped out, pulling the door shut behind him.

"You've seen," he said, peering closely into Royce's eyes, "how it is—up there?"

"Yes."

"Whatever you can do," Mr. Rosen continued in his nasal voice, "to help them on their way . . . things are going from bad to worse there. And let me tell you—" the man hesitated, lowered his voice and rasped, with some urgency now in his tones, "the police have been around . . . keeping an eye on things. If you know what I mean."

After a pause, Royce said, "I know what you mean."

"You'd think they have enough to do," Lev Rosen said bitterly, "stopping the riots of grown men who are, in the only way they know, expressing their anger and frustration over life, such as it is for them. But no, they prowl our poor streets, dragging in desperate little offenders—"

The man surprised his listeners with his passion and his volubility.

"Ah well," he said, stemming his lashing against the un-fairness of life as experienced in The Ward, "anyway, you'll do what you can for the lady and her brood?"

"We will, indeed," Royce said with some fervency. "I'll be back before I set off for home—the Territories, that is."

As they made their way along the streets of The Ward, their progress was watched, it seemed, from dozens of door-ways and windows, perhaps hundreds of eyes. Never had Meg's second-best dress seemed so ostentatious; never had Marlys's outfit seemed more ridiculous with its rustling taf-feta lining, gimp and tucks, and horn buttons. Meg half looked for a thrown apple or orange to send their hats flying. But there may have been kindness in the sunken eyes and appreciation that one of their group had received encouragement and help at the hands of the visitors. News traveled fast in The Ward.

Nevertheless, the ladies, at least, breathed easier when they passed into more respectable streets, and their steps slowed. Once again it was an enjoyable afternoon stroll. The Graphophone, when they passed it this time, seemed like something from another planet, an empty, useless mishmash of wires and tin when compared to the stark, simple necessity of a bottle of milk.

"You'd think," Marlys said eventually, breaking into their private silences, "the Children's Aid Society and Fresh Air Fund would do something."

"You read John Kelso's report in the *World*," Meg said wearily. "He's a police reporter," she explained to Royce. "He's appalled at the number of children who are doing nothing worse than begging, sleeping in the streets, and pilfering and so on, who are imprisoned heartlessly. I think eventually he will stir up some real help for these children."

Royce Ferguson looked down at the heart-shaped, earnest face of the speaker and moved into place beside her. Marlys, outmaneuvered, ungraciously fell into step with Becky, obviously finding her too juvenile to be worthy of communication and so falling silent.

As the conversation between Royce and Meg moved from the streets of Toronto to the homesteads of Saskatchewan, Wildrose in particular, Marlys glowered. Reaching their own gate, finally, she (gracious again) invited Royce and Becky in for Sunday afternoon tea. After a moment's hesitation, the invitation was accepted.

Once inside, Marlys seated their guests in the parlor, turned to the hall to remove her hat, elbowing Meg aside. For a moment the sisters were reflected in the hall mirror—

the one tall, slim, imperious, her hair golden, her eyes blue, her color flawless; the other a trifle shorter, a little thinner, her hair a shade darker, her eyes hazel, her manner honest and straightforward.

"Go get the water boiling and make the tea," Marlys said crisply, pinching her cheeks as she leaned into the mirror. "Tell Wilda we'd like to have some small sandwiches and some of that cake she's hoarding in the pantry."

Meg, shrugging, turned toward the kitchen, while Marlys hurried back to the parlor.

"Becky, my dear," she suggested, "I'm sure Meg would appreciate your help," and Becky, as amiably as Meg had, turned toward the kitchen.

Seating herself beside Royce Ferguson, Marlys said, "What an interesting afternoon! Thank you for sharing it with us; we saw a section of town that I haven't seen since coming to Toronto. I think it would be admirable to spend one's strength in doing something for people like we saw today."

"You do, Miss Shaw? Er—Marlys," he said, correcting himself when Marlys shook her golden curls at him and called him "Naughty!"

"Now," Marlys added in a confidential manner, "tell me all about Wildrose. What a beautiful name; it just conjures up a scene of rustic beauty. I'm sure I should just love Wildrose!"

"You would?" the rather bemused man asked. "I know your sister is greatly attracted to that sort of life, but you—?"

Marlys laughed. "I take that as a compliment, Royce. I'm much tougher than I look! Perhaps," she said idly, "Meg has forgotten the terms of our parents' will. Or perhaps, rebelling against them, she finds the life of a pioneer attractive, purely as an alternative."

"Alternative?" Royce was puzzled but interested.

"Yes, an alternative to the restrictions placed on each of us by our parents' will."

"Will? Restrictions? Do I have any right to ask what you mean? But you did bring it up—"

"I think you should know . . . for dear Meg's sake. Meg, you see, is bound by our parents' will to stay single until she is 21, as I am. She, of course, is not yet 18 . . . I will soon be 21, have my inheritance, and be free to do as I wish with my life."

"I should think, Miss Shaw . . . Marlys," Royce made the change because of Marlys's arch look, "that any husband would happily take on the responsibility of caring for his wife and providing for her."

"But it's Harley's *duty* to see she doesn't marry for three more years. His permission—if it should be asked—would have to be denied—for Meg's own good. I should think it would be a hard decision for any suitor to make, asking his wife to give up her inheritance *and* headstrongly going against her guardian's advice."

Marlys concluded sweetly, "Harley and I strongly feel our responsibility for our little sister and want to guard her carefully."

Meg and Becky wheeled in the tea cart to find a curiously quiet Royce and a bubbly Marlys. If Royce gave Meg a long, heavy glance from time to time, she didn't see it. If his departure was abrupt, she put it down to weariness. But when Royce said, at the door, "Marlys, perhaps you'd take dinner out with me tomorrow evening," Meg understood.

Marlys's whirl around the room—once the door was closed behind the departing Royce and Becky—her skirts flying, her curls likewise, her eyes shining, and her mouth smiling triumphantly, Meg understood. Just what Marlys had done or said she might never know, but that it had been done, been said, was as certain as though it had been spelled out. And as chilling, in Meg's heart, as the tea turning cold in the bottom of Wilda's china cups.

9

When the door had closed behind her departing visitors, Amanda Lamb, with her tall young son's arm around her waist, was urged toward a chair at the side of the table.

"Read it, Mama! Read it!" five voices urged, while little Kerry, not to be outdone, piped, "Wead it . . . wead it!"

With trembling hands Amanda opened the letter and removed a single sheet of paper and numerous bills. Silently, breathlessly the family watched as she counted them. Then, eyes ashine, she looked at the tensely absorbed children.

"It's almost enough," she said. "With what we've saved, it's almost enough."

The children's faces were a mix of happiness and disappointment; obviously they had hoped for better news.

"Each of you go get your money, darlings," Amanda said now, correctly interpreting their reactions. "We'll count it and see exactly where we stand. But bless our dear papa! He's brought our dream so much closer to reality!"

The children scattered. Ammie reached into the ancient range's warming oven, removing a lard pail, and bringing its contents to the table. Jake hefted the wood box, retrieved a bag, and drew several well-worn bills from it. Joe and Josie, working together as always, lifted a corner of a mattress and brought forth a much used and abused velvet pouch, ran with it to the table, and dumped its contents in its own separate pile before their mother. Amanda, when the children were involved with their own funds, reached into the bosom of her dress and withdrew a small, flat pocketbook.

Silently, the bills were counted and stacked; patiently the coins were counted and piled.

Amanda raised her eyes to the anxious faces of her children. "Just a few more weeks, darlings, and we'll have it all. Can you hold steady a little longer? I know you can. I know you will."

"We will, Mama! We will!" chorused the group that was bunched around the frail body of their mother.

With high spirits the money was regathered and hidden away again. Ammie brought out the cupboard's odd assortment of bowls, Josie brought spoons, and Freddy set the bottle of milk in the middle of the table and produced two cups, placing them at his mother's place and little Kerry's.

"Let's all have a cup of milk tonight, to celebrate," Amanda urged, but Jake, Ammie, Freddy, Joe, and Josie—though the last two cast longing glances at the pearly liquid—stoutly resisted the temptation.

"You need it, Mama, you and Kerry," Jake reminded not only his mother but all of them. "You know what the doctor said—"

"Milk and fresh air!" the children chorused.

"Freddy takes care of the milk part," Ammie said, "and Wildrose will take care of all the fresh air we can breathe."

"And Faithful—don't forget Faithful!" chimed Josie.

"Yes, Faithful will provide lots of lovely rich milk, for all of us. In the meantime Papa milks her and sends us the money to add to our train fare."

Speaking of Faithful the cow and Papa reminded them that they hadn't, as yet, read Jacob's letter. Now a clamor arose and Amanda opened the penciled sheet of paper.

"My dear wife and children," she read, while the children settled quietly onto their chairs and stools. "This will introduce Mr. Royce Ferguson, one of my neighbors. I'm so glad I can send along this money for your fare. I hope and pray you will all join me before snow comes next fall. The crop looks good. The garden is doing well, and I will have a supply of food in the cellar: pumpkins, potatoes, turnips, and more."

The sunken eyes of Jacob Lamb's family brightened with anticipation; the stew on the stove, the older ones knew, was mostly water and potatoes, with a few carrots shredded in, and a handful of macaroni. But there was bread brought home by Amanda from the grand house where she worked in the kitchen. And milk for Mama and Kerry. And before many weeks had gone by they would be on their way from the smoky city and crowded tenement to the clean skies and plentiful food of Wildrose.

There was much to be thankful for. Amanda, when she had finished the letter, bowed her head, thanked God for their food, and they fell to eating with a will after Ammie had carefully ladled supper into their bowls and shared the bread according to their size and their need. There was enough for breakfast, and Mama would bring more tomorrow.

When the skimpy meal was done and Ammie and Josie were washing and wiping the dishes and Amanda was preparing Kerry for bed, a knock sounded on the door.

It was Lev Rosen, as it usually was. No one from their former life, before Jacob left, knew of their straitened conditions and their willingness to save money to hasten the day of their departure.

Into Freddy's hands Lev Rosen placed three apples, as

he often did—apples or oranges or perhaps a bag of bakery buns. Never much, but it was faithfully—and stubbornly, because of Amanda's resistance—given.

And usually—because of Amanda's broken thanks—Mr. Rosen hurried back to his own apartment. But tonight he looked over the heads of the watching children to ask, "That man and those young women, was it all right to send them up?"

"Yes! Thank you, Mr. Rosen. They are friends . . . the gentleman brought news of Jacob. We're going to make it yet, Mr. Rosen! And much of it is thanks to you . . ."

And again Amanda Lamb's eyes misted and her voice thickened. Mr. Rosen quickly backed out followed by a chorus of thanks from the watching family.

"*Dear* Mr. Rosen," Josie said in such an imitation of her mother's oft-stated phrase that they all laughed, Josie turned red, and they looked longingly at the fruit.

"Not tonight!" Freddy said authoritatively, and they all sighed. "These are beauties. I'll shine them up and sell them tomorrow. With the money I'll buy six more—if I watch I can get a good deal—and sell those, buy some more, and so on all day. Tomorrow night the fund will be even bigger!"

"I'm so proud of all of you," Amanda said. "It'll be worth it all—very soon!"

And with that note of cheer the little family went to sleep on the two beds in the other room and the sagging couch in the first room. But the bedding was clean, the mother's kisses were tender, and their dreams were filled with visions of a log house in a green and flourishing land where a cow named Faithful munched happily, a dog named Bounder wagged a welcoming tail, and frothy cups of milk overflowed at each heaped plate.

10

When Miss P whirled out of the parsonage yard and turned her rig toward home, she was, for once, blind and deaf to the charm of Wildrose.

Being a young woman with a broken heart when she had moved with her parents to the parkland of Saskatchewan, her pain had not abated through any human ministration. Her parents had done their best, even going so far as to remind her that here, in the beckoning West, were many men who were lonely and whose hearts were as empty as hers. Phoebe could barely believe she was hearing such tactless and empty comfort and mourned her dead love painfully and silently.

Only the coming of spring had stemmed the winter of her grief. Spring and summer and fall—each in its way and in its time—had ministered a healing balm and planted in Miss P a passionate appreciation for this her adopted home. Birdsong lifted her from melancholy to music; chinooks melted the inner icicles as well as those hanging five feet long from roofs; the incredible fragrances that began with the tiny violet and crocus of early spring perfumed her days until the pungent fresh-straw smell of autumn was smothered by winter's first snow.

Perhaps Miss P's reputation began in those days. Certainly before long she was regarded as somewhat of a character by those who knew her best and were kindly disposed toward her or as a slightly "touched" oddity by those who knew her little and cared not a whit to know her better. Now, well past the prime of life and comfortably situated (a little money influenced opinions!), she was accepted with a patient and understanding smile by most people of the district and well loved by a few. To Miss P it mattered not a bit, and she went her own way, marching to a drumbeat heard only by herself.

Today, engaged with the problem of Jacob Lamb and his refusal to let her be neighborly, her mind, for once, overlooked the joys she usually absorbed as if by some mysterious osmosis.

The common dandelion, for instance, which most people declared to be a weed and a nuisance, Miss P knew as a valuable plant. No longer, it seemed, did anyone consider that its roots were a fine laxative; no one, even the poorest among them and thirsting for the coffee they couldn't afford, cared to dry its roots and use them for a coffee substitute. Miss P was still known to offer it to visiting guests, only to be quickly thanked and refused in favor of the ubiquitous tea. Miss P had learned not to offer tea made from the sweetly fragrant and abundant red clover. Occasionally someone, most notably Pastor Victor, would, with staunch confidence in her wisdom, agree to a cup of tea made from the hips of the wild rose; a teaspoon of them, steeped in a cup of boiling water for 10 minutes, made a refreshing brew.

Perhaps only Miss P, of the entire area, knew that the leaves and flower buds of milkweed are delicious boiled; such tidbits of information caused conversation to languish and eyes to roll and did Miss P's reputation no good whatsoever.

Prickly lettuce, called the compass plant because its leaves point north and south, grew abundantly across mainland Canada; its one-to-six-foot plants would have fed an army, Miss P thought, if anyone had cared to try it. And fireweed, its spiky magenta blossom so pervasive and so beautiful, had a use no one suspected; not only could the inner pith of the mature stalks be eaten raw, but the young shoots, boiled, tasted like asparagus. Many a half-starved homesteader and his family, Miss P thought, sighing, would have found their diet enhanced with a little ingenuity.

Once, in midsummer, a newcomer to the district had dropped by to borrow the use of Miss P's lathe to turn out a new grub hoe handle he was whittling by hand. To his amazement the spare but spry woman, built rather on the lines of a whippet, was on her hands and knees, digging—of all things!—couch grass. Now since couch, or quack grass, grew rampantly and tenaciously in cultivated fields, gardens, pastures, and along the roads and is known to be one of the most difficult weeds in the world to eradicate, the man could not be blamed for watching with considerable astonishment as Miss P calmly gouged out another rootstock and added it to many already in her basket.

"I say," the man stammered, overwhelmed by the spreading mass of grass that grew, as far as he knew, clear to the tundra and perhaps beyond, "isn't that rather a hopeless task?"

Miss P, holding up her trowel and wiping the perspiration of the warm day from her sunburned brow, had said pleasantly, "I'm going to grind these rootstocks into flour."

The surprised man, with an inward guffaw of unbelief, turned homeward to a supper of rabbit stew without the benefit of any kind of bread, because of an empty cupboard (and an empty head, Miss P thought crisply, knowing the situation and having already loaned the family a sack of good wheat flour to help fill the gap until their own small field could be reaped and their grain ground).

Now, with a plate of carefully covered raisin cookies beside her, made of good Red Fife wheat flour, Miss P had no eyes for the bounty flourishing around her and no ears for the music of the parkland that issued from fence post, bush, tree, and sky.

The Golden Rule might, just might, she had said to her pastor, work in reverse. But before she tried that, she determined to give it one more try. Reaching under the snowy linen that covered the cookies, Miss P chose one and chewed it thoughtfully, found it perfect, and urged Old Mag to a faster clip.

After the gentle jog behind an aging Old Mag, she came to the Lamb homestead and turned in. Pulling to a halt beside the stoop, Miss P thrust out a bony ankle and long foot for the buggy step, got down agilely, and went to the door. There was no answer to her knock.

Knowing the house would be unlocked (the newcomer had lived in Wildrose long enough to know *that*), Miss P—honest to the core and reluctant to push open a shut door—knocked extra hard, perhaps striking the knob in her enthusiasm. At any rate, the door swung open.

"Yoo-hoo," yodeled Miss P. There was silence, of course; the man was obviously not in the house.

The log house, which Miss P had been in during the lifetime of Jacob's uncle, was a large square. One half was the living area; the other half had been divided into two smaller rooms—bedrooms, most likely.

Furnished as the elder Mr. Lamb had left it, it could have been comfortable enough—with a woman's touch.

Miss P struggled with herself; wisdom lost and enthusiasm won.

Setting down her plate of cookies among a hodgepodge of laundry and dirty household utensils and dishes, Miss P turned to the range, tested the water in the reservoir, found it warm, and filled the dishpan hanging from a nail on the wall. Locating a brown piece of soap, Miss P, with an available rag, worked up a lather. Then, happily, she plunged a handful of dirty dishes into the suds and commenced soaking and scrubbing the accumulation of food from them.

So pleased was she at finding a need and filling it, that Miss P began to hum, then to sing.

> *"Give me a faithful heart,*
> *Likeness to Thee,*
> *That each departing day*
> *Henceforth may see*
> *Some work of love begun,*
> *Some deed of kindness done,*
> *Some wand'rer sought and won,*
> *Something for Thee, "*[*]

she caroled gladly, and never heard the door creak open.

"Just what is going on here?"

The man's voice was cold, very cold. His eyes even colder. Miss P, startled by the interruption, jumped and only barely caught a soapy cup before it slipped out of her grasp.

"Why," she said slowly, "I came to bring you some cookies."

"And stayed to become a busybody!"

[*]S. D. Phelps, "Something for Jesus."

"Not at all," Miss P said mildly. "My desire, you see, is to apply the Golden Rule—"

"Well apply it somewhere else. I'm doing just fine, Miss Partridge, and I'll thank you to remember it."

"I wanted to help—"

Again the icy voice from the man leaning against the door jamb: "I'm getting along very well, and I'm doing it without the help of any neighborhood mother hen!"

Miss P's angular frame stiffened and her faded eyes snapped. (Longsuffering was not one of Miss P's spiritual fruits that flourished naturally.)

"Well, I'm sorry, I'm sure," she said with as much dignity as she could muster, under the circumstances.

Miss P left the house through the door the man was holding elaborately open. But not before she wiped the table, emptied the dishwater, wrung out the dishrag, dried her hands on a gray bit of sacking that served, apparently, for a towel, and hung the dishpan on its nail behind the stove.

"Mother hen indeed!" she couldn't help but fume as the door slammed behind her. Hoisting her voluminous skirt, she stepped into her buggy with unusual vigor, turned the startled Mag, and whirled from the Lamb yard.

Miss P knew she was no spring chicken, but mother hen!

On second thought, she didn't mind it all that much. As always, she was about her Father's business. That it had led her into someone else's "nest" had been coincidental.

And—perhaps not so well hidden as she thought—Miss P harbored a deep-seated desire to "mother" someone. Not quite accepting the fact, still Miss P knew that, buried deep within her, the childlessness of her existence ached sorely.

Miss P sighed, thinking of this her latest attempt to do unto others. Perhaps this time she had let her zeal get the best of her. It wasn't always easy to be as wise as a serpent and as harmless as a dove. There should be some middle ground; perhaps mother hen was it.

Back home, Miss P sat in her spotless house and drank the tea she had brewed in an attempt to calm her nerves, collect her thoughts, and make her plans.

"It has to work!" she said firmly, being an unshakable believer in the perfect reliability of Scripture. "If that Jacob Lamb won't allow me to 'do unto him as I would have him do unto me,' " she paraphrased, "he'll just have to do unto me as I would have myself do unto him."

That, somehow, didn't quite express what Miss P had in mind, and she sipped thoughtfully for a few minutes.

"Like I said in the first place," she concluded briskly, "maybe it works in reverse. There's more than one way to skin a cat!"

And with these homely words of wisdom, Miss P narrowed her eyes, drummed her fingers, and laid her plans.

11

At the breakfast table in the Ferguson home, after the younger members of the family had scattered to school and Roland had departed for the newspaper where he set type and Mrs. Ferguson had returned to the kitchen to supervise the "help" in getting Monday's wash under way, Royce stirred his coffee thoughtfully.

"Becky," he said finally to the sister who was beginning to clear the table, "tell me about the Shaw sisters."

Becky set aside the flatware and dishes she had lifted, preparing to take them to the kitchen and the first round of dishwashing for the day, and took a seat across from her brother. Her round face quickly hid the grin that threatened, and her quickly lowered eyelids shut out the flash of comprehension that had lit them at her brother's words, as if to say, "Aha! Just as I thought. But I won't spoil it by teasing."

"They've only been here about six months. They came from England, of course, as you can tell by their accent, where they were under an aunt's care. Now they live with their brother, Harley."

"How old are they—the girls, I mean?"

"Well, Marlys is about 21, I think. Meg is, er, 18." Becky, loyal to her friend, was honest, too, and added, "Or almost. But she is very mature, Royce!"

Royce smiled faintly at his sister's defense of her friend.

"I feel a little uncomfortable asking—but what do you know of their financial status? That is," he continued, noting Becky's confusion, "their inheritance from their parents?"

"I don't know anything about it," Becky said. "They always seem to have money to spend, but they are not lavish about it. Harley has a good job, but I think he may have gotten so well set-up so early in life because of an inheritance. He seems to take care of his sisters."

"They are accustomed to every comfort, of course," Royce said as though thinking aloud.

"No more than we are, Royce. If they have money, they don't mention it, at least Meg hasn't. At any rate I don't suppose it's much. But why all these questions, Royce?"

"Just . . . asking."

"Would it make any difference, if Meg has money? I'd think if a person fell in love—"

"Money or no money, it doesn't matter to me," Royce was quick to say. "But there might be certain conditions that would make a great deal of difference."

Becky waited for some further word of explanation. When it was not forthcoming and Royce continued to stir his coffee in a mechanical manner, she changed the subject.

"Royce, I'm serious about wanting to go back with you. Please—listen to me!"

Royce, with a start, put down his spoon, picked up his cup, took a sip, found its contents half cold, set it down, and gave his attention to his sister.

"I believe you are," he said with some surprise. "You can't know what you're talking about though."

"I know as much as you and Neal knew, when you

started out!" Becky defended herself stoutly.

"It's not a change to be made lightly, Sis. You can't think of it like going on a vacation or anything like that. It would mean a commitment—to whatever came up. Summer's work would be heavy—"

"I'm strong . . . healthy . . . willing!"

"And when winter comes, it's really something to be reckoned with, the isolation, I mean."

"You and Neal would be there."

"But if you found you couldn't take it and wanted to come back home, a winter trip might be out of the question, Becky. First of all, there's no guarantee you could even get through to town to the railway station. And then the train could very well be delayed or not come at all. That's the way it is. And there'd be no hotel in Meridian where you could stay and wait. It would mean a freezing trip back to the homestead . . . another try another day."

"If I go, I'll stay." When her brother looked skeptical, Becky said, with some passion mixed with embarrassment, "I want to stay permanently! I hope . . . well, I hope I would find the person I would marry and become a homesteader myself. I mean it, Royce." Becky finished her speech with a pink face but an unflinching gaze.

"Whew!" her brother said, half smiling to ease the tension. "I believe you've got the spunk to do it."

"I'm not a baby, Royce. I know my mind. Please talk to Mum and Dad! I can be ready to go when you are. Two weeks, did you say?"

"Sooner, if I can finish my . . . business."

Becky looked at her brother's noncommittal face as he stared down at the cup he was slowly turning in his hand.

Bold as only sisters can be, she finally asked, "Then are you looking for a wife?"

Royce smiled briefly at her brash query. "There's certainly no one in Wildrose. And I'm 28, little sister, and not getting any younger."

"And you have your house now and your place. And there's all those lonely winter days, right?"

"Right. It would take a very special sort of person to fit in. Perhaps it's a feeble hope that any girl would take it on—take *me* on. And especially in the length of time I've got to see to it. Well," Royce took a deep breath, "even so, we'll see about you coming back. You'll love Wildrose, Becky. And even if I get lucky . . . blessed . . . enough to find someone to share my life with me, there's still Neal. He's just 25 and not even looking, as far as I know. So you may get to be an old maid destined to keep house for one or the other of your brothers."

"Oh, Royce! Thank you! I'm going to start counting on it, getting things ready and so on, and leave it up to you to talk to Mum and Dad. It won't come as any surprise to them; I've been talking about it ever since we knew you were coming back."

And Becky, as rambunctious as she was roly-poly, gave her brother a hug.

"And you," she finished hesitantly as she turned toward the kitchen, her hands once again loaded with dirty dishes, "are taking—*Marlys*—to dinner?"

"It seems wisest, Becky," Royce said briefly, and Becky sighed, disappointed and, somehow, troubled.

A block away, in the morning room of the gingerbreaded red brick house, Monday's wash was also under way.

"Wait!" Marlys commanded, and Meg, about to take an armload of soiled clothes downstairs, paused.

Marlys was pawing through drawers, turning some of them out on her bed, sorting certain garments into heaps, dropping a few into what seemed to be a discard pile on the floor.

"Take these with you," Marlys said, loading several garments into Meg's arms and studying others critically. "Go . . . go!" she said impatiently to the hesitating Meg.

"These aren't things you've been wearing . . . poor Fanny is overworked as it is. Couldn't some of them wait? Some of them are winter things, aren't they?"

"Just take them, Meg! I have my reasons. As for Fanny, she's paid to do washing, isn't she?"

Meg, face a study of suspicion, incredulity, and despair, took the clothes to an already overworked Fanny. The girl, no more than 15, staggered under the load, and Meg's heart went out to her. Fanny's little red hands—which Meg had seen swollen with chilblains during the winter—seemed too childish for such a massive task; her shoulders too narrow for the burden life had thrust on her.

"I'll help," Meg said and felt that Fanny's smile was thanks enough for giving up her morning.

Wilda studied the situation when she next passed through the washroom. "What's this? Why in the world has Marlys chosen this morning to clear out her closet? It would have been much better if she had sent down only a few of these. Surely there's no hurry to get them all done at once."

Wilda hurried upstairs, to stem the flow of clothes if she could.

"What's going on, Marlys?" she asked, stepping into the room shared by her two sisters-in-law and looking at the heaped clothes and open drawers.

"I need to work on my wardrobe," Marlys said shortly,

her head inside the closet. Backing out, she held up and scrutinized a two-cape mackintosh. Handsome and well trimmed, made of a fine wale diagonal serge and lined throughout with plaid, its detachable cape featured a velvet collar, and all, insofar as Wilda could see, in perfect condition.

Marlys frowned critically. "There are some that have an opening—an 'aperture' the clerk calls it—with a flap that is very handy if one should need to raise one's skirts."

"Raise one's skirts?" Wilda could be pardoned for sounding, and looking, confused. And more than a little disapproving.

"Skirts! Like when one has to walk through mud or across farmyards."

"Farmyards? Not likely, Marlys, here in Toronto."

Marlys tossed the mackintosh onto the bed and turned again to the closet, emerging now with an elegant suit that Wilda knew was made of imported cheviot. Its jacket with its fly front featured the newest sleeves and cuffs, and the entire suit was lined with black silk serge and trimmed with the smallest of pearl buttons. With two fingers Marlys held out the full skirt and studied its taffeta lining and velvet binding.

"Black?" she mused, "for traveling? Not good. It would show dust like everything. But it could be packed." And she tossed it toward an open trunk.

Marlys held up and studied a suit styled with a bolero cape of very fine quality, with collar and lapels appliquéd and elaborately embroidered, lined with silk and trimmed with green moiré ribbon, the cape featuring four rows of soutache with its herringbone pattern.

"Hmmm," Marlys said, holding the brown and gold mixtured suit against her face and studying the effect in the mirror. "What do you think?" she asked a bewildered Wilda.

"I think you better put it away and do something constructive with your day," Wilda said firmly. "I could use some help with the marketing. Daisy seems to have awakened with a fever, and I don't see how I can get away."

"Marketing," Marlys said coolly. "I'm really not any good at picking out turnips and leeks. And it's not one of my favorite things to do."

"It has to be done," Wilda reminded her somewhat frigidly. "And you eat, too, you know."

"But perhaps not for long." Marlys, holding a summer suit of washable crash to her cheek, mused, "This blue linen trimming on here does go well with my eyes. Now this outfit might just make a good wedding dress—if one were in a remote and probably unfashionable area, don't you think?"

"Wedding? Remote area?" Wilda, who had not come down from her children's room when the Fergusons had come in for tea, could make no sense of the conversation.

"The marketing, Marlys?" she asked with a sigh.

"Meg is much better at it than I," Marlys said. "Besides, she is much more the outdoors type than I am. Not that I can't . . . and won't . . . do what is necessary to—"

Marlys gave her sister-in-law a sharp glance, left her sentence unfinished, and said instead, "Meg will probably be happy to do it for you."

Wilda, knowing them both, agreed and reluctantly took Meg from her washday duties, providing her with a list, a shopping basket, and a purse.

Just before Meg turned to get her hat and her gloves, Wilda asked, "Do you have any idea what Marlys is up to? She's going through all her clothes and talking strangely about wedding dresses and remote areas."

Meg's face, flushed from the steam, lost some of its color. "I—I think I might have some idea," she said faintly and turned and stumbled toward the hall without further explanation.

Wilda shrugged and sighed and turned toward her ailing child; Fanny struggled to the clothesline with the first basket of laundry; and Meg walked through brilliant sunshine and might as well have been sleepwalking through the dark.

It was as though she was jolted from a dream—or a nightmare—when Meg heard her name called and saw Mrs. Ferguson and Becky sorting through the potatoes at the open stalls where Wilda did her vegetable shopping.

Becky turned aside, pausing at Meg's side to greet her friend cheerily.

"Guess what! Royce says I can go with him! And he's going to talk to Mum and Dad for me. Oh, Meg, I wish you could go too."

Becky's excitement wavered and her voice faltered as she remembered . . .

"Don't count on it," Meg said flatly. "*I'm* not."

"Oh, Meg, I had hoped . . . that is—"

"So," Meg said thoughtfully, not misunderstanding her friend's hesitation, "it's pretty well settled on that end, too, is it?"

"Royce—that is, he didn't say much, of course, and then to no one but me. But his decision, *if* he's made a decision, seems to have something to do with, well, with yours and Marlys's inheritance."

"Inheritance?" Meg asked blankly, fingering the same apple until the clerk's watchful eye seemed to indicate she might be bruising it.

"Is there some . . . some *secret*, maybe a clause or something that would demand that you be an old maid or something?" Becky asked anxiously.

"There's nothing. It must be something else. The legacy for all of us was the same, except that Harley got twice as much as Marlys and I. But that's fair enough. He was to make a home for us until we married. He couldn't have bought the house and got married and still have us come on over if he hadn't had Papa's money. His is about all gone, he says, but his job is going well and there's no worry over money, for him *or* us."

"Well, I don't understand it, I'm sure," Becky said doubtfully. "There must be some reason—"

"Reason, Becky? There's always been a reason, every time I find something I want to have or do. It's Marlys. And really, Becky, it's understandable. Just look at us. Marlys is ever so much more . . . attractive. Who wouldn't look at her first and most?"

Becky looked at her friend with anguished eyes. "Oh, *Meg!*"

"I'm quite used to it," Meg said, blindly choosing an apple that had a bad spot on it and dropping it into her basket.

"But you wanted so much to go," Becky mourned.

"I don't expect to," Meg said, and there was a finality in her voice that put an end to the conversation. "No, I expect it's all signed, sealed, and decided. Or will be very soon."

Becky watched her friend move on down the stalls and bit her lip and fought her tears. Meg's tears would not be stanched, and they splashed on the small basket of strawberries in her hand like a passing and inconsequential spring rain, changing nothing.

12

In spite of the children's objections, Amanda had saved a cup of milk for their cereal in the morning, setting it on the windowsill for the night. In the morning before the children were up she started the porridge, more a thin gruel than anything else, and sat down at the table with a pencil and piece of paper to write to her husband in the faraway Northwest Territories.

Dear Husband:

We were so happy to get your letter and learn that you are in good health. Thank you for sending the money. We counted our funds and find we lack only a small portion of the amount needed for all of us to take the train to Wildrose. Jake continues his work at the stables for Van Damm Dray and Hauling and is growing into a strong young man of whom you may be very proud. I'm sure he will be able to be a big help on the homestead. Ammie is growing into a fine young woman, tho' I worry about her. At times she comes home from the Worbliss house with unexplained bruises. She shrugs off my questions but as she is growing thin (along with getting tall), I am sure, for one thing, they do not feed her the good noon meal they promised when I took her there to ask about the work in their kitchen. They have a boy who is about 18, and my worries seem to center around him. But Ammie assures me everything is all right. Darling Freddy works like a little Trojan, doing anything he can, and he comes home most days with a pocketful of change. He sells things, makes things, helps people, sweeps out the corner barbershop. My concern, which I have mentioned before and which I know you share, is that the schooling of all the children is being neglected at this time. I try, after work and on the weekends, to get them to their books, but I fear I don't have very good success. For one thing, my dear, it seems they all regard *me* as the child with themselves as the parent! They do look after me very well, and I'm sure I am feeling better. We all dream of the day when we will be with you, work hard, grow healthy and strong, and be done with this wild scramble to keep body and soul together.

Joe, at nine, is no longer the little boy you left two years ago. And Josie, a year behind, is still his shadow. Between them they have a corner where they sell papers. That's so one of them can always be with Kerry, who is such a good little girl. My heart grows sad at times to see her cooped up here in these two rooms, but we shall soon be where we have a yard and animals and plenty of good food and *our own place.* It is enough to keep us all working hard and saving all we can. As you know, I've begrudged so much as the cost of a stamp and therefore appreciate Mr. Ferguson's kind offer to take this letter for me.

It is almost time to scatter to our jobs, and so I

must get the children up. You can rest in the knowledge that we are all in good health—

Here Amanda paused, stifling the cough that seemed to plague her more all the time and then, with a sigh, continued her letter.

—and as happy as we can be, without you. The hope of being together very soon keeps us all going.

Love from
your wife and family

Jake was rousing from the uncomfortable old sofa in the corner of the room, sitting up, rubbing the sleep from his eyes, running a hand through his dark, auburn-tinged hair.

"Do you really think we can be ready to go in two or three weeks, Mama?" he asked quietly as his mother folded the letter she had been writing.

Amanda's head, once the bright color of Freddy's and which showed up, in one degree or another in all her children, turned a loving look on this eldest son, on whom she had learned to rely.

"Actually, Jake, we have enough for our fare. It's just that we can't go in the makeshift garments we are wearing. All of you have either outgrown or outworn your clothes. Fortunately Josie has been able to wear Ammie's and Kerry is falling heir to Josie's. But they are so worn, and all of us need shoes. Papa won't have these things for us when we get there, and we'll need to be prepared not only for this summer but a bitter winter."

Jake nodded; they all knew about winter, having nearly frozen as well as starved in their ramshackle apartment. The blizzards of the north were legendary; they would need to be prepared.

But her words brought hope into the young man's eyes and he rose with greater alacrity than usual, slipping into his threadbare pants and shirt and pulling on large, ill-fitting boots that the man in the secondhand store had said were "Hard Knock" shoes. Well, he'd had enough hard knocks to do a lifetime; Jake felt he'd work night and day and do it happily, if it were for his own father and on their own place. The thought was enough to send him into the other room to rouse the children and urge them up and into their clothes. Remembering the bitter mornings during the past winter, Jake hoped fervently they would be gone before another such desperate season.

It was during the winter that Mum had developed the sickness that lingered on into the warm weather and that kept her so thin, her poor body racked with the grinding cough that worried them all so much. And how could she continue to work as hard as she did? Jake ground his teeth in his frustration and near despair. They just *had* to get Mum away before she collapsed from weariness, overwork, and poor nutrition. Did Papa know how bad things were? Jake found no opportunity to add a line to his mother's letters and never had a stamp to call his own.

And the children weren't much better off. They, too, were overworked and suffered, he was sure, from the lack of proper things to eat, though Freddy did his best where milk was concerned. And Mr. Rosen—whom they all learned to love in spite of his unattractive manner of dress, hunched body, and a voice that sounded like a rusty door hinge—had consistently added to their barren larder by his offerings, usually fruit or vegetables, and always healthy, if somewhat stale and limp.

"Get up, all of you!" Jake said now, more gruffly than he meant to, and the children crept, like field mice, to their clothes and to the table.

Amanda served up the gruel and divided the one cup of milk among them, adding a skimpy few grains of sugar. The bread, though without butter, had been toasted.

It was Joe's turn to stay with Kerry, and so it was also his turn to do the dishes and make the beds.

"It's nice today, Mama," Joe said. "Can I take Kerry for a walk and maybe sit for a while on the stoop and watch people?"

"When you get the work done, Son. You'll be sure," the mother's voice was anxious, "to watch Kerry carefully? Never let go of her hand? And you, Kerry, hang onto your brother! If you don't, I can't let you go outside at all." With this warning and the earnest nod of Joe and the big-eyed "I'll be dood" from Kerry, Amanda kissed each child, put on her hat and mended gloves, and left for the house, a very large house, on the other side of town where she worked as laundress. It meant car fare, and Amanda reluctantly doled out the meager five cents going and coming. But it was too far to walk; her health would never have stood it, and it would have meant another hour or two away from her little family. Besides, if she was lucky, Mrs. Sylvester, a kind soul at heart, would put something in her hands to take home with her—bread, a bit of sugar perhaps, tea at times, and, occasionally, bacon or a meat bone.

Arriving at the Sylvester mansion, Amanda went directly to the basement where the tubs were set up and where the family's accumulation of laundry came tumbling from a chute. It was a busy household with many servants and, clearly, a dozen or more children. And all of them, it seemed, changed from the skin out each day, and bedding was changed twice a week.

First she gathered the clothes that had been drying on the lines strung around the basement, folding, sorting, damping down all that needed to be ironed. Then she turned to the task of filling the tubs, shaving the soap, sorting the clothes that had to have—not only a clean, well-folded look, but a sweet smell. There must be no scum, no stains, no sour odor. Any buttons popped off in the wringer must be caught and reattached at mending time.

Mrs. Sylvester was old-fashioned; though the house was electrified, she had a deadly fear of the power. Consequently she looked askance at electric washers, with their noise, their gears ever turning, their tendency to shiver and shake.

And so Amanda was as familiar with the household's Improved Wayne Washer as with her own tin washbasin at home. Made of sturdy ash with corrugated staves and bottom and with wringer attached, it was undoubtedly better than a washboard, and for that Amanda was grateful.

The largest washing, the maker of the Improved Anthony Wayne Washer promised, could be finished in three or four hours if directions were followed. "Suds need not be removed every time," said the instructions, "but can be used until they become too dirty. But always add hot water, soap, and compound and keep the machine well filled."

The trouble was, they also directed "Do not put over five shirts or four sheets at a time into the machine." Consequently, Amanda's three or four hours stretched to seven or eight, many days.

She knew the recipe for Anthony Wayne Washing Fluid by heart: "Take one pound of potash, one ounce of salts of tartar, one ounce of ammonia. Place the potash into a large crock or earthen vessel, and pour a gallon of hot water

99

slowly into this vessel. Wait until this cools, then add the salts of tartar and the ammonia, and when all is fully dissolved, bottle the fluid for use. All of the ingredients," the manufacturer assured, "could be bought at any drugstore at a cost not to exceed 25 cents."

But Mrs. Sylvester, being proudly "old-fashioned," still insisted on use of her favorite Fels Naptha for certain needs. There was "Wool Soap" for woolen items; there was the lye for bleaching, the blueing for whitening, as well as the "sad" irons to deal with.

Amanda's spell of coughing during her excitement the day before had weakened her; more than once she leaned, breathless, over the steamy tub or wringer, or iron (four pounds for the No. 1, five and a half pounds for the No. 2, five and three quarter pounds for the No. 3, and none of them as heavy as the charcoal lighter at six and a half pounds), and the Geneva Hand Fluter weighing four and three quarter pounds. Ironing—a fearsome job.

Finally, dragging herself into her jacket and preparing to leave, Mrs. Sylvester had called to her. Going upstairs, Amanda gladly received the packet the lady of the house placed in her hands with considerable compassion, knowing a little of her laundress's family and their needs.

In the car, Amanda peeked inside the bulky package and recognized the materials of several pieces of clothing. With a grateful sigh, she reclosed the package, knowing one problem, at least, had been solved. The clothing of Donna Sylvester, also 13 but a larger, sturdier build than Ammie, would provide for Ammie the much-needed wardrobe she needed for the trip and relieve the overburdened Lamb purse. Already washed and ironed, the dresses—wisely Donna's most practical ones—would be put aside for that magical moment, now within sight, when they would leave

Toronto forever for the blessings of Wildrose. Amanda tried to conjure up the fragrances the name implied but breathed only the garlic reeking from the weary laborer at her side.

Ammie, who put in four hours a day in the Worbliss kitchen, had finished the breakfast dishes (and, in the doing, had shamefacedly rescued and eaten half a piece of buttered toast and most of a discarded egg), scrubbed the floor and shined the stovetop, and headed for the cellar with a pan to get the potatoes and bring them up for peeling. Reluctantly she descended into the basement's gloom . . .

In the half light, Ammie was startled when a shadow emerged from behind the door. Her involuntary shriek was smothered by the soft large hand that quickly covered her mouth.

"Gotcha! Think you're so smart . . . always scooting to my mother, you little drab!"

Ammie struggled, filled with consternation and, as the grip of the young man tightened, fear. The more she fought him, the closer he held her, obviously enjoying the mastery of his will and his strength over hers.

This wasn't the first time Wilkie Worbliss had waylaid his mother's scullery maid. More than once a well-aimed kick had enabled her to slip past him. And usually she had avoided confrontations, if she could, and had only to put up with sly leers, lascivious pinches, and whispered promises . . . threats.

Today she had thought the 18-year-old had left the house. There was no way she could scream for help, and she wasn't sure Mrs. Worbliss would be at all sympathetic if she did manage to attract attention.

Holding Ammie between himself and the wall, Wilkie swiftly replaced his hand with his equally soft face, seeking to press his lips to Ammie's mouth. Instinctively Ammie acted; as the fleshy mouth met hers, her keen teeth bit and bit sharply. With a shriek and an oath, the boy released his grip, and Ammie slipped out, up the steps into the kitchen, to lean, white-faced and trembling, against the door she slammed shut behind her.

The startled gaze of Mrs. Worbliss took in the small shivering form, heard the gasping breath, and noticed the absence of potatoes. Stepping to the door she pushed the girl aside, glanced down, heard her son, half muttering, half sobbing below, and said, "Get your things. You're done here, my girl!"

Ammie could only comply. Mrs. Worbliss counted her wages into her hands and thrust her from the back door and Ammie never knew if the woman's eyes were blazing because of anger at her helper or her son.

More dazed than hurt, Ammie walked home. As the fear and revulsion waned, her misery increased. So near to having enough money to make the trip, and now this!

Ammie was home and waiting when her mother arrived; even the clothes, lovely though they were, and needed, could not stem the torrent of tears that flowed now in her mother's arms as she told the story, explained the bruises, revealed the torment.

"There, there," Amanda soothed. "You should have told me, Ammie. I wouldn't have put up with it a minute, not a minute!" Even as she said it, Amanda's mind was thinking dumbly of what would undoubtedly put a delay on their plans.

Peace and calm had been restored somewhat when Jake came home, bringing a dime's worth of minced meat and a sack of aging vegetables. Ammie, drying her tears, insisted that her mother sit down, take Kerry on her lap, and rest while she and Jake put the stew—this one with *meat* and quickly turning savory—on the stove.

Josie brought in the coins from a successful paper-selling day and a darkening bunch of bananas that Lev Rosen had given her as she passed his door. The anticipation of a good supper, along with their newly kindled hope of leaving for the Northwest very soon, lent an aura of cheer to the small, cheerless rooms. Jake found himself whistling "The Old Oaken Bucket." Ammie, spirits lifting, soon hummed along. Joe and Josie sat together on the window ledge, reading the funny papers from the day-old paper Josie had brought home and actually laughing.

But the whistling stopped abruptly, the humming faded, and the laughter ceased when the door slammed open and Freddy burst into the room, collared by a burly, red-faced policeman. With his free hand the man of the law held triumphantly aloft, before the gaping and startled eyes of the family, a bottle of milk.

13

Miss P walked through dew-drenched quack grass to her hired man's shack. The sun, not yet blazing full force, looked kindly on the thinning hair, angular frame and face, bony wrists and equally bony nose, and added its own luster to the faded kind eyes. Kind but full of purpose.

Watching his employer's approach and catching the gleam of her eyes, Luther, quite properly, muttered, "Uh-oh!"

Lily turned from the dishpan of breakfast dishes and said, "That kind of day, eh?"

" 'Fraid so."

"It's always interesting," Lily said, drying her hands and going to the door to let Miss P in.

"Coffee?" Lily asked.

"No thanks, dear." Miss P, when on a crusade, had no time for nonessentials.

Getting right to it, she said, "Luther, there's a shingle sort of jutting up, beside the stovepipe."

"I've seen it. Been that way for years. Isn't leaking around there or anything, is it?"

"I want you to loosen it."

"Fix it, you mean?"

"No, loosen it."

Luther studied Miss P's face.

"Well," he said, sighing, "I suppose I better do it, or you will."

"That's the plan, all right," Miss P said mysteriously. "And Luther, do you have something you could do on the other side of the place?"

"Hmmm. You want me gone, is that it?"

"Just for a while, Luther," Miss P said with an apologetic smile.

"Could go to Meridian, I suppose. Got things I could do there. Do you want that Lily should go with me?"

"Not necessarily. Lily, I believe, will find plenty to do *in the house.*"

"How long do I have to be busy *in the house?*" Lily asked, mindful of her garden and its burgeoning weeds.

"You'll know, Lily. You'll know. And you, Luther, could you be on your way in, say, an hour from now?"

"Fine with me," Luther said, shrugging, and walked with Miss P to the shed. There he located a ladder, placed it against Miss P's house and, with a hammer and screwdriver in his pocket, climbed to the low roof and pried and fiddled around until he was confident the shingle could be said to be loose.

"Better not rain," he said over his shoulder to a watching Miss P.

"Not a chance," Miss P said calmly.

Luther climbed down and hefted the ladder.

"Leave it leaning against the shed," Miss P instructed, and Luther did so.

"Anything else?"

"Set the pail of whitewash in on my table, please."

Luther brought in the pail to find a newspaper on the table, ready to receive it. He had thoughtfully brought along a brush.

"Thank you, Luther. One more thing. Bring that can of pine tar and set it here," and Miss P pointed to the steps to her kitchen. "There, that's it, I believe." And Miss P looked at her watch, glanced down the road, and urged Luther to get on his way. "And by the way, bring Mr. Lamb's mail back with you."

Shortly, Lily, watching curiously from her window, saw Miss P exit her own house, linger on the step until, head cocked, she seemed to hear a sound that sent her scuttling to the shed and the leaning ladder.

Clearing the bush and coming into view on the road was a lone man in a buggy—Jacob Lamb, Lily could discern as he came closer. But that was not unexpected. Mr. Lamb, every Friday at this time, almost without fail, passed by on his way to Meridian and the mail.

Miss P was acting very peculiarly indeed. She had picked up the ladder, turned herself, and was tottering toward her house. The top of the ladder swayed to and fro, almost overbalancing the deceptively frail figure. Lily knew a fine performance when she saw one, and Miss P, angular legs akimbo at the knees, elbows jutting, sashayed back and forth and round and round as if at the whim of the ladder, yet ever moving toward the house, in as fine a performance as achieved by any Shakespearean actor.

Mr. Lamb's mouth dropped open, and he slowed his rig.

Miss P's gyrations and perambulations carried her in a devious back-and-forth pattern across her yard as she strove mightily to balance the long ladder. Finally, just about the time Jacob Lamb's buggy reached her gate, the entire structure collapsed. And Miss P with it.

It was more than any man could stand. Whirling into her yard, Jacob Lamb cried "Whoa!" and leaped from his still rolling buggy and across the intervening space to the prostrate woman.

Miss P was rising, not too shaken it seemed, to arrange her skirts and straighten her disarranged hair, tucking it back into the bun at the nape of her neck.

"Miss Partridge! Are you all right? This is too heavy for you! I'm surprised you didn't get your man to do it for you!"

"He's gone," Miss P managed. "And my roof," she pointed a wavering finger toward the stovepipe and the jutting shingle, "needs fixing . . . and it might rain."

An unabashed Miss P said this even as the man's unbelieving eyes took in the vast expanse of a perfectly cloudless sky.

"You old fraud!" Lily said admiringly to herself, shook her head, and went about her business, *inside* of course.

Outside, the drama continued. At Miss P's direction the gullible Mr. Lamb picked up the ladder, took the tools Miss P handed to him, climbed to the roof, and in a few minutes had the shingle securely fastened in place. Miss P, standing on the bottom rung, handed up the tar and brush, and Mr. Lamb dabbed the sticky goo in and around the repair job.

Standing down again, his dirty hands before him, Miss P suggested he step inside for a wash. While Mr. Lamb was drying his hands on a snowy towel, Miss P was looking up, studying the area where the stovepipe entered the room.

"That spot, of course," she mused, "will have to be repainted."

And when she had pointed it out, Mr. Lamb supposed he could see a rain blotch.

With a sigh he opened the pail, stirred the contents, stood on a chair, and whisked a fresh coat on the offending spot. Climbing down, Jacob Lamb asked, elaborately and, it must be admitted, a bit sarcastically, "Anything else, Miss Partridge?"

"Well, now that you mention it . . . it's so nice, you see, to have help in time of need. There are some things, of course, a woman just can't do—"

With a suspicious face Mr. Lamb dusted the tops of Miss P's windows, brought a heavy crock from her pantry, worked with a stubborn window until it moved up and down easily, and climbed, finally, down into her cellar where, at her instructions called down from her position on her knees beside the trap door, he rearranged a few boxes of vegetables and swept under them, set a mousetrap, and finally climbed out, a gleam of laughter in his eyes.

"Miss Partridge," he began.

"My friends all call me Miss P," Miss P said demurely.

"Miss P, I give up! Before you work me to death—I surrender. I don't quite know how you got me into this fix, but I get the point. I'm quite sure you're going to want to pay me back for all I've done for you."

"It's the proper order," Miss P agreed with a bob of her head, bustling to the stove and pouring the boiling water from the kettle into a waiting teapot. "Now you just sit down and rest while I get the tarts from the pantry."

Soon Mr. Lamb, expansive over a good deed well done and enjoying baking such as he hadn't tasted since he left Ontario, was telling Miss P all about his absent family. Each child was named, one by one, and described with loving, lonely words. Amanda was introduced and their dreams and plans shared with an attentive and sympathetic new friend.

Finally Jacob Lamb pulled out his watch and with an exclamation leaped to his feet. "My trip to Meridian! I've let the time get away from me!"

"Sit down, Mr. Lamb," Miss P said, "and tell me more. Your mail will be along soon, with Luther."

And Jacob, dazedly, sat. *I don't know why I ever held out against her,* he thought, *when giving in is so rewarding. I'm sure she's going to want to know what she can do to help me get my place in shape for Amanda and the kids.*

"And now, Jacob," Miss P asked, passing the lemon tarts, "just how long do we have until your family arrives?"

14

It was a brooding Meg who watched Royce Ferguson and Marlys out the door, down the walk, onto the sidewalk. Royce had offered a glowing Marlys his arm; they made a handsome couple.

Becky, standing just behind Meg's shoulder and equally as brooding, muttered, "He had to have a new suit for the occasion. Said he needed it, hadn't had any new clothes to speak of since he left home; said he was tired of overalls and boots."

The suit, of black cheviot, featured the round-cut sack style as opposed to the square-cut, and it was double-breasted ("Never mind that it cost 50 cents extra," Becky continued to mutter), showed to advantage the manly figure, and the derby was worn at a jaunty angle.

"He bought another one for Neal," Becky reported, watching the pair out of sight. "A suit, and other clothes, to take back."

"Are they the same size?" Meg asked.

"Neal is a little shorter, a little slimmer. But Royce has always sort of taken charge of him. Of course, he's younger than Royce and has been traipsing after his older brother ever since I can remember. Even traipsed out West with him."

"Well, he didn't traipse back here with him, did he?"

"No, but then Royce probably told him he had to stay; one of them had to, I guess. I've always been closer to Neal, probably because he's nearer my age. But," Becky said thoughtfully, "come to think of it, it may be that he and I always got along better. I miss him . . ."

"Never mind. You'll be seeing him soon, Becky. When are you leaving?" Meg had been told that the exuberantly happy Becky was to be allowed to go with Royce.

"Not sure. Just between you and me," and Becky sighed and cast a last glance at the couple now almost out of sight down the block, "I think he's going to get himself a wife and when that's settled, he'll take off."

Meg let the curtain fall into place and flung herself onto the sofa. "And I . . . ," she whispered, "wanted it to be me."

"Oh, Meg!" Becky said compassionately, seating herself by her friend. "And I wanted it to be you! We could have had such a great time! Don't give up the idea!"

"Well, I have. You don't know Marlys, Becky. She gets what she wants. And it seems she wants Royce."

"But," Becky asked wisely, "does she want the life of a homesteader's wife?"

"Maybe she does. Maybe this is one affair she'll go through with. We'll just have to see how it works out, won't we?" Meg's tone was flat, her eyes hopeless. It was clear she had no expectation that her own dream—a future in the Territories, Wildrose in particular—would come true.

"Come upstairs with me," Meg invited, rising.

The two girls made their way to Meg's and Marlys's room; here Meg silently pointed out all the signs that Marlys was considering not only Royce as a husband but Wildrose as her destination. The trunk was open to disclose Marlys's wardrobe to be half packed; shoes were lined up in

111

a row, chiffonnier drawers were hanging open to reveal their contents well sorted over.

"I declare!" Becky said, awed. "I never saw such confidence! How does she do it?"

"I never learned. I've seen it work, over and over again, but haven't got it figured out. No doubt," Meg said a trifle bitterly, "I haven't got the proper equipment for it." And Meg looked pensively at herself in the mirror. "I've always known I was, well, sort of in Marlys's shadow. But she was older, and a leader, and it seemed natural. Certainly it never mattered before."

Meg put her hands to her cheeks and her hazel eyes, pained and embarrassed because of it, threatened to fill with tears. Whirling from the mirror she took a deep breath. "Is there life after Royce? Of course, there is. But oh, Becky, I'll miss *you* so very much!"

And the two friends clung together momentarily, then wiped their eyes, and Meg began to sort through her belongings, wanting to share some special treasure with Becky, to be remembered by when they were far apart.

Meg was in bed, reading, when Marlys came home. Shutting the door behind her, a pink-cheeked and very self-satisfied Marlys unbuttoned her gloves and tossed her hat onto the closet shelf.

"Couldn't have gone better!" she reported, though Meg hadn't asked . . . hadn't needed to.

"Do you know what you're doing?" Meg asked, looking from her book with troubled eyes. "Life in the bush—Marlys, it seems so unlike you."

"But Royce is worth it," Marlys said.

"You've thought that before. That Jackson Ironwood back in England—you let him think he was worth staying there for, but you left when the time came."

Marlys's laughter was scornful. "He wasn't half the man Royce is! There's something about that manly, outdoor, earthy type that just sends shivers all over me!"

"You'll shiver all right, in that 50 below weather."

"Oh, Meg, don't be so gloomy. Why, one would think you were jealous! Surely not—a child like you couldn't imagine a man of Royce's caliber would give you a second look!"

Not a second look, Meg thought with a pang, *but a first—he did give a first!*

Marlys—vibrant, sparkling, breathless, and rapt as she studied her reflection in the mirror—had no doubt about her ability to get what she wanted.

Catching sight of her sister's speculative expression in the mirror, Marlys turned swiftly and cried, "And what makes you think I'm not serious about this, Missy?"

"Perhaps you are, Marlys. For Royce's sake I certainly hope so. Not everyone has time to play games."

"Games! I mean this! You'll see! And Meg," Marlys offered kindly, beginning to get ready for bed, "you can come visit us. Now won't that be something to look forward to?"

Visit Marlys and Royce? Never! Meg buried herself in her pillow and though she sternly shut out any daydreams, her night was filled with visions of spreading green bush giving way to neat cabins from which smoke lifted lazily toward the sky . . . axes rang and cows ambled to a neat log barn, bell jangling and cowbirds riding piggyback. Meg could hear it . . see it . . . even the dog on the porch rising to meet her, tail wagging a glad welcome . . .

It all seemed so real. But reality, when she woke, was much different.

15

Amanda rose to her feet, her hand going to her breast. Jake stepped to his mother's side; the other children watched, wide-eyed.

Officer Riley, known to all the inhabitants of The Ward, marched Freddy to stand in front of his mother. Red-faced and squirming, Freddy didn't meet Amanda's eyes.

In spite of the pulse that beat in Amanda's white temples, she spoke quietly. "What is the meaning of this, Officer?"

"Go on, lad, tell her!" The policeman shook the small, somehow shrunken form. The red curls jounced, and Freddy's face tightened, but he did not speak.

Amanda turned her attention to the officer again. "Has Freddy gotten in some kind of trouble?"

"Some kind of trouble? I'd say so! Tell her, lad!" Again the man shook the boy.

"It's . . . it's the milk, Mum," Freddy said in a half-whisper.

Amanda studied the downcast face of her second son. "I think you better tell me about it," she said to the officer. "And I should think you may let him go now."

Officer Riley loosed his hold, but Freddy continued to

stand where he was, at the officer's side, and in front of his family.

Holding the offending bottle before him—exhibit number one—the man said, "Caught the little scalawag pinchin' this here property. Caught him right and proper, I did. And it ain't the first time, I'm bettin'. Someone's been gettin' away with milk on several streets for quite a while now. I had me suspicions and kept an eye out. It's this young feller-me-lad, all right, all right!" Officer Riley was clearly triumphant.

"Freddy?" Amanda's voice was sorrowful.

Freddy squirmed and cast an agonizing glance at his mother's pale face.

"Freddy?"

"You needed it, Mum," Freddy said in a low voice, and Amanda's face, if possible, whitened still further. She closed her eyes momentarily, feeling her responsibility in her son's need to provide for her.

Amanda drew a quivering breath and Freddy, looking up, said wildly, "I druther go to jail than take back what I did!"

Officer Riley, well acquainted with life in The Ward, and a father himself, must have felt his heart soften. He looked around at the signs of poverty, noted with a sharp eye the bone-thin figure of the mother and the clean faces and garments of her poorly fed, poorly dressed children, and sighed. Nothing would be gained by taking the boy in. But, he reasoned wisely, the little nipper would have the fear of life behind bars thrown into him!

"I'm not takin' ye in *this time!*" he growled in a voice that made the boy wince and the mother catch her breath with hope. "But let me tell yer somethin'—if I ever catch you up to any shenanigans again . . . it'll be prison for sartin!"

Amanda knew it was possible. She knew children as young as six had been sent to prison. A boy just Freddy's age had been given a three-year prison sentence for stealing a lamp.

"Thank you, Officer Riley," the frightened mother managed, "thank you so much. I think you may be sure Freddy won't steal anything again—ever. Freddy?"

Freddy scowled ferociously and dug the toe of his boot into the floor.

"Freddy?"

"All right!" Freddy promised savagely. "Not even if you and Kerry are dyin' of hunger!"

The mother bit her trembling lip; the officer drew a ragged breath, blinked, and offered one or two more growled threats for good measure and turned and left. But not before he had set the milk bottle on the table.

Amanda reached out to the boy caught in such a terrible web and didn't know how to fix it. "Freddy," she managed, "what you did wasn't right . . . but your reason for doing it—oh, Freddy—"

But Freddy evaded the hand held out to him so beseechingly and turned and fled into the other room where he flung himself down on a bed, and though no sound escaped to be heard by his silent and stunned family, the iron bed frame shook as the thin body, undernourished as it was, heaved with an anguish no child should feel and a load no child be asked to carry.

Ammie crept about fixing the meager meal. Amanda, coughing and wishing she wouldn't—for the sake of the boy curled into a ball in the other room and knowing no way to help her other than illegally—rocked Kerry and wondered despairingly if the disease she suspected racked her so pitilessly might even now be fastening on the sweet little body pressed against her with such terror.

And indeed they were all frightened. They knew how very close Freddy had come to being dragged away from them.

"We've got to get away," Amanda told the children as they sat up to the table. "We can't take such chances. Now let's lay some plans—"

Amanda would work the rest of the week. "That should give the Sylvesters time to find someone else. And Josie and Joe can both go out, and Ammie will stay and look after Kerry."

At the surprised looks on the faces of all other children, Ammie flushed and her head drooped and Amanda said firmly, "Ammie has put in her time at the Worbliss place; she'll be home until we go. You, Jake, give notice tomorrow and plan to be done the end of the week. Freddy—" Amanda spoke clearly, aware that Freddy was hearing, though he hadn't come to the table, "will stay here with Ammie."

"Oh, Mum," Jake said, "he won't get in trouble again. And the barbershops count on him sweeping up. He'll have to give notice too."

Amanda hesitated. Even needing the money so badly, she hesitated.

"My fear is not that Freddy won't do what's right . . . now," Amanda said. "It's something else that's worrying me. Every household in The Ward is alerted to the fact that some busy—but well-meaning, I suppose—lady from the Children's Aid Society is on the alert on our streets. It's so newly formed, I suppose they are filled with zeal right now; it'll fade before long, as any other efforts to help have done. But," Amanda shivered, "if she gets an idea you children are uncared for . . ."

The thought seemed too dreadful to express. The little ones looked at her anxiously, and even Ammie and Jake were solemn.

"They put the Dodge kids in the orphanage," Joe said suddenly. "Oh, Mama! Let's go right away."

"We can't go to the orphanage!" Josie squeaked. "And we don't want Freddy to go to prison! Let's go be with Dad!"

"We will," Amanda comforted and sat counting their money long after all but Jake were in bed.

"Can we make it, Mama?" he asked, watching his mother's white face and hearing her repetitious cough.

"We must," Amanda said. "Listen to me, Son. If something happens to me, you must take the little ones and go by yourself. Do you understand?"

Jake's face grew still.

"Do you hear me, Son?"

"I hear you, Mama."

"Do you understand?"

"I—I understand."

"And you must do it quickly. The Society would separate you . . ." Amanda's eyes reflected the unspeakable horror of her meaning.

"I won't let that happen, Mama. I promise you I won't let that happen."

Jake's thin shoulders—too laden for anyone his age—straightened. And his eyes—too haunted for any boy this side of manhood—filled with purpose.

"I'm counting on you to remember." And Amanda, relieved, coughed her way to bed and through the night.

16

Miss P awoke to a prayer. It seemed the proper time to begin her experiment—and the only way.

At bedtime the night before, Miss P's mind had been too full of questions—raised during her preparation for teaching the Worthy Warrior's Sunday School Class—to voice her prayer or even bring it into focus properly. But now, having slept on the idea and finding it a good one, she was ready.

"Dear Lord," she prayed, "today I plan to bake a saskatoon pie for Pastor Victor. And, of course, this is the day I stop by and chat with Hubert and Harry. And then, dear Lord, I shall stop at Jacob Lamb's and do what I can to help that dear man get prepared for his family to come. Now, dear Lord, I'll do all these things unless You 'suffer me not.' "

Miss P's unusual wording was the direct result of the Scripture passage she had been studying before she went to bed. It was a scripture she had read many times before, but never had she been challenged by it as this time. And Miss P, being Miss P, couldn't let it go unsolved.

Now, having outlined her proposed itinerary for the day, Miss P kept her eyes closed and waited. She waited and listened. It must be admitted that her mind strayed for a few guilty moments to the pie and the thought that she might just have enough berries to make one for Jacob Lamb too. And then thoughts of Hubert's and Harry's sprightliness in spite of their aging bodies brought an inadvertent smile to her lips, until once again she fixed her attention on listening and, she hoped, hearing from the Lord.

But after five minutes or so, Miss P figured she had allowed enough time for the Lord to speak if He were going to do so. Somewhat disappointed at what she thought was a poor beginning to her experiment, Miss P arose to face her day, trusting she would hear as she went.

But while the tea steeped and the oatmeal bubbled, the Lord didn't speak, although Miss P listened attentively.

Sipping her final cup of tea, Miss P turned to her lesson notes and the scripture that had stirred her to action. She followed Paul and Silas through Syria and Cilicia, Derbe and Lystra, Phrygia and Galatia. But she came up short again when the "Spirit suffered them not" to go into Bithynia.

Miss P didn't quibble with God's plans and purposes; she didn't question His perfect will and His right to it. But His wish for involvement in everyday affairs had never been so apparent to her before. She suspected God's direct involvement in her day-to-day plans was woefully lacking.

Washing up her few dishes and setting out the ingredients for the pie crust she would make, Miss P thought about God's word-of-mouth instructions to His people in olden days. "Come thou out and all thy house into the ark," He had said to Noah. "Get thee out of thy country . . . unto a land I will show thee," had been His command to Abram. The child Samuel had heard his name called three times, and when he responded, "Speak; for thy servant heareth," God had said, "I will do a thing in Israel . . ." and outlined it. These things and more God had clearly told people to do.

And now, with "the Spirit suffered them not," Miss P was face-to-face with divine intervention so specific that it *forbade* a planned course of action. "Don't do that," God had said in essence, and He had changed the route of Paul's missionary journey.

Ever alert to her Christian privileges, Miss P had determined to check it out; it seemed a reasonable thing to do. And so she had laid out her plans for the day and had given the Lord an opportunity to forbid them or approve them. She had asked and she had listened but to no avail. Not as yet, she thought as she went to the well to pull up the pail dangling there and into which she had placed yesterday's berry picking.

"Morning!"

It was Luther, on his way to the barn with a milk pail swinging at his side and two wise cats trotting behind, tails aloft in the brisk early morning air.

Greeting her hired man cheerily and spending a few minutes in conversation with him about the needs of the homestead, Miss P thought, as she so often did nowadays, "I'm so blessed! Uncle Roscoe has made it possible for me to keep Luther on and also include Lily's services from time to time . . . leaving me free for things I've always wanted to do."

Pausing to listen, mindful of her "experiment," all Miss P heard was the bawling of the cows awaiting milking and the birdsong that charmed the day into waking with good humor. Enjoying it all, Miss P came to with a start, took her berries, and went back to her house, waving at Lily who was already getting her first clothes on the line. Lily, a freethinker, did not conform to Wildrose's Monday washday schedule, to the disapproval of some—Dolly Trimble in particular. But it bothered Miss P not at all; in fact, she rather admired Lily's carefree independence.

Miss P tried not to be too distracted by her pie making, which was, after all, routine except that she decided to include gooseberries in the filling. "It will stretch the berries to *two* pies," she told the dozing Tom Bigbee, "and give them more zing." Saskatoons were, after all, very mild. Areas of the world more blessed with fruit might turn up their noses at saskatoons, she realized, but here in the bush, to winter-starved appetites, they were a treat fit for a king's royal table.

Miss P had her own unique way to judge the heat of her oven. Opening it now she thrust in her bared arm and began counting; at 20 she could stand the heat no longer and deemed it properly hot for the pies. (Bread, not demanding as hot an oven, was ready at the count of 30.)

Pinning on her hat, Miss P paused again to listen. But God wasn't saying anything insofar as she could tell, and she sighed. Her class next Sunday was sure to ask if one could expect God to do today as He had done in times past. Did one just blunder through one's day and tasks? It was a question Miss P couldn't overlook.

So Miss P rather regretfully loaded the buggy that Luther had obligingly brought to her door and set out on her rounds saying, "I really did want Your will, Lord, not mine. But—I'll keep on listening."

Jogging along through the beautiful morning, Miss P spied, in the bush at the side of the road, a flash of orange. Stopping the rig she got down, plowed through the burgeoning growth, once cut back but growing quickly, to locate and pick the lovely and usually hard-to-find tiger lily.

Hurrying now to assure its freshness on delivery, Miss P reached the parsonage.

"Do come in, Miss P," Ellie Victor greeted their parishioner cordially.

"Can't today," Miss P caroled and placed the pie, running succulent juices, into her pastor's wife's hands.

"And here," she said, producing the lily, its head abob and its fragrance making the moment a special one indeed, "this is for Pastor's desk."

"Oh," Ellie said, burying her nose in the blossom, "he'll be so pleased. It's been a tough week."

"Dolly on the rampage again?" Miss P asked, knowing that Dolly's face had flushed last Sunday and her mouth tightened when Pastor Victor had asked for favorite hymn selections and he had chosen Moira MacTavish's request for the triumphant "We're Marching to Zion," rather than her choice, "The Sands of Time Are Sinking."

Ellie sighed but said only, "This will speak volumes to him."

And Miss P went her way gladly, though sobering quickly to hear what the Lord might be telling her to do—or *not to do* today.

Hubert and Harry Runyon, older and ornerier than ever, to Miss P's relief (she dreaded the day they were beyond fussing at each other, a sport she and all of Wildrose enjoyed as much as the elderly brothers), greeted their old friend with cries of joy.

"Has Sarah had the baby yet?" she inquired after she had taken a seat at the side of the cold heater, where Hubert and Harry reigned summer and winter, their loneliness gone forever now that Willie Tucker had married their great-niece Sarah and come to live in the look-alike house a hundred yards away, one of two that the brothers had built when they came to homestead not long after the middle of the century. With their wives, Virgie and Bessie, they had been among the first to burrow their way into the bush, to find the spot of their dreams and to wrest a living from the rich black soil that had turned to the plow blade when their first small field had been cleared.

"Not yet," Harry said, "any day now."

"We're workin' on names," Hubert informed an interested Miss P. "If it's a boy, we're sure Sarah will want to call it Hubert Harry—"

"Harry Hubert!"

"And if it's a girl," Hubert continued, ignoring his brother's huffing and puffing, "it will be—"

"Harriet!"

"What do you think of Huberta, Miss P? Or maybe Hubertina?"

And so the happy jangling proceeded until Miss P took her departure, well content that things were normal with Hubert and Harry. What a relief it had been to the district when Sarah and her small son, Simon, had arrived to bring order and hope out of chaos and despair for the two elderly men.

"And now," Miss P said to Old Mag, Tom Bigbee being absent, "we'll go see Jacob Lamb. Unless, Lord, You 'suffer' me not." Not at all certain now that the Lord was all that concerned with her routine, Miss P sighed, slapped the reins on Old Mag's back, and soon pulled into the Lamb yard.

A smiling Jacob came from the barn and invited his guest into a house newly tidied.

"It's really not all that bad, Jacob," Miss P said, eyeing the main room critically. "Just . . . just sort of *empty* looking, if you know what I mean."

"When Amanda and the tribe get here, they'll take care of that."

"The curtains need doing up, Jacob." And Jacob nodded agreement.

"I think I'll just make a few cushions for these chairs. That would please me very much," Miss P said, and what man could deny a woman such pleasure?

"And the bedding?" Miss P asked, more delicately. "If it's like mine after a long winter, it needs washing."

"I suppose so," Jacob admitted.

And so they spent a pleasant half hour drinking the coffee that had Miss P's jutting nose wrinkling and eating a slice of the saskatoon-gooseberry pie, which did indeed have "zing."

Jacob gallantly helped Miss P up into her buggy. "My Amanda's life will be much richer, when she gets here," he said, "for your friendship."

Miss P's faded eyes sparkled; it was all the thanks and encouragement she needed.

"Just as soon as the cushions are done," she said now, "I'll bring them over and take time to work on those quilts."

"Thank you so much," the man said warmly. "I'm sure you are heaven-sent, though it took me a long time to see it."

"I'm sorry about that, Lord," Miss P said apologetically when she was on her way again, "but he seems to think You sent me. I didn't deceive him intentionally, I assure You!

"Now I'm going to go by and comb Grandma Dunphy's hair free of tangles, Lord," she continued. "Unless You have something else You want me to do."

Aside from the clip-clop of Old Mag's hooves, silence reigned.

About that time she noticed that Old Mag was limping. After careful scrutiny it seemed advisable to turn in home and not continue to the Dunphy place. Pulling in, she was alarmed to hear a voice calling, "Help! Help me!"

The sound seemed to be coming from the Boggs's yard. Miss P alighted and hurried toward the sound of the cry. Around back, the plump form of Lily turned a pitiful face toward her rescuer.

"I've broken my ankle," she wailed.

Miss P knelt in the grass and comforted the injured woman. "Where's Luther?" she asked, knowing Lily needed to get in out of the sun, already showing the effects of its midday burning rays.

"I don't know! I've been lying here for . . . for *hours!*"

Miss P was sure it hadn't been that long; neither was she sure the ankle was broken. But that it was badly sprained and very painful was certain. Miss P helped the trembling Lily up, steadying her, urging her to lean on her, and slowly Lily hippety-hopped to her house, inside, and into a chair.

"I better get Anna," Miss P said, with reference to Anna Snodgrass, the nearest thing to a doctor the community had.

"What's going on?"

It was Luther, home at last. He soothed his wife, saddled up his horse, and went for Anna. Miss P bathed Lily's hot face and brought a pail of cold, sparkling water from the well and gave Lily a refreshing drink. Anna, on arrival with her nostrums and potions, took over, and Miss P went home.

Sitting disconsolately in her house, Miss P felt she had come to the end of her schedule with no appreciable difference in this day than any other.

"Well, that's the end of that," she said with finality to Tom Bigbee.

But, honest as she was, Miss P pondered on what she could possibly tell her class about God's guidance. After a lifetime—a long lifetime, she thought ruefully—of serving the Lord, it did seem inappropriate for her to be so sadly lacking in knowing and doing His will!

God, insofar as Miss P could determine, hadn't said yes or no all day.

But she rose to the occasion when Pastor Gerald Victor came by and invited him in warmly, bustling about making tea, setting out fruitcake and serviettes, and sharing with him her concern for Jacob Lamb and her relief in regard to Harry and Hubert.

"I wanted to tell you," Brother Victor was saying feelingly before Miss P realized it, "how I appreciated the tiger lily. Ellie had it on my desk when I got home from my discussion with, er, one of my flock."

At Miss P's raised eyebrow he added hastily, "A very dear member but one who needs extra, er—"

"Handling," Miss P said with her usual frankness.

"Anyway, the lily gave me a lift. God knew I needed some sign today that someone cares."

"See here, Pastor! I can't let you think it was an inspired act on my part."

Pastor Victor smiled fondly on his parishioner. "Oh, but I'm certain it was," he said.

Miss P looked bewildered. "But surely I would know."

"Not specifically, my dear Miss Partridge," her pastor said after a quick glance at her earnest face. " 'A man's heart deviseth his way,' you know, 'but the Lord directeth his steps.' "

"Proverbs 16:9," Miss P murmured, wondering how she could have forgotten.

"Well, then," she said gropingly, "those Sunday School papers I took to Hubert and Harry—"

"I'm sure they thanked the Lord for them."

"And arranging to help Jacob get his dirty quilts washed

before his wife and children get here—"

"A gift from God, I'm sure," the pastor said, stirring his tea.

"And being here when Lily needed me . . . not going on to the Dunphy's after all! Mag's limping, changing my plan completely! God said, *'Don't go there'!*" Miss P's tired eyes were alight with understanding. "Pastor Victor! God 'suffered' me not!"

Pastor Victor had never seen anyone as happy about God's closed door.

"It's bound to happen occasionally," he admitted and verified, "In all thy ways acknowledge him, and he shall direct your paths."

"Proverbs 3:6," murmured Miss P. "And that's just what I'll tell them."

"Tell them?"

"The Worthy Warriors," Miss P explained. "I'll be ready for them when they ask. And they're bound to ask."

"Knowing them, I'm sure they will," her pastor said. "And knowing you, I'm sure you will."

Miss P settled back with her tea. Seeing her eyes lit with purpose, her pastor felt quite sure she could hardly wait for another day and another challenge from the Word of God.

17

On Wednesday evening Royce came for supper. At Meg's invitation, Becky accompanied him.

The children were in bed, Fanny was laboring in the kitchen, and Meg was putting the last touches to the table when the doorbell sounded. No use going . . . Marlys, dressed and waiting, swished to answer it.

"Good evening!" she cooed. (Meg wondered how Marlys could coo anything as mundane as a greeting.) Royce's deep voice answered and Becky, apparently handing Marlys her hat and gloves, escaped and slipped into the dining room.

Here she greeted Meg hesitantly. Full of her plans to leave, thoughtfulness forbade any enthusiasm in the face of her friend's disappointment.

Perceiving the dilemma, Meg prompted, "Are you getting things together, Becky? How are the plans progressing?"

"*My* plans—fine," Becky answered. "Royce's—I can only guess, but I'd say they are moving right along."

And both girls listened to the light laughter issuing from the parlor where Marlys had escorted Royce. Meg sighed, tweaking a serviette into place.

"Do you know when you're leaving?" she asked.

"No, but I'm betting we'll know very soon—maybe even before the night's over." There were low voices in the parlor, intimate voices.

"Royce has been picking up things he and Neal need, and Mum has rounded up household items that she doesn't need any more and wants them to have. She thinks they'll feel more like it's home if they see things from here around them."

"That's nice," Meg murmured, scarcely listening, her ears hearing and her heart understanding the distant murmurs. It wasn't the first time, by any means, that she had been an onlooker to Marlys's affairs of the heart. That she could be serious this time seemed impossible. This time!

Now Wilda and Harley joined them, and soon they were all seated at the table and Fanny was bringing in the boiled beef dinner that was Harley's favorite.

"Tell us about your place, Mr. Ferguson," Harley invited.

"Call me Royce, sir. Well, my brother Neal and I feel fortunate to have found homesteads side by side. We each have our cabins up—" Royce glanced apologetically toward Marlys. "They're more than a homesteader's typical cabin, I believe, having a large living area and the remaining half divided into two smaller rooms. Typical arrangement, I suppose, and ideal for heating."

"Mighty cold, of course, much of the year."

"Yes indeed. One has to be prepared. There's wood aplenty, of course, and if one has plenty of supplies, and er . . . pleasant company, life can be good."

Royce's tone implied, to Meg's thinking, that the isolation and deprivation would fade into insignificance if one were happily and contentedly married.

Marlys must have thought so too. "It sounds like a cozy

little nest," she breathed.

"Well, yes—it could be just that." Royce turned meaningful eyes on the glowing Marlys. Becky made a face at Meg who, in spite of mixed anger and anguish, almost choked with laughter.

"I don't believe dear Meg quite appreciates the possibilities of such a life," Marlys said. "It would demand all the womanhood one has, but what a reward—just to feel the satisfaction of a day's work accomplished, a night's rest deserved, and tomorrow's dreams beckoning!"

Even for Marlys this was a fanciful high. Meg found her sense of humor deserting her and a sense of futility rising.

"Tell us about your brother," Harley suggested, perhaps a little taken aback by his sister's impassioned prosing.

"Neal? A good worker, strong, healthy, dedicated. Much in love with the bush and happy to be there. Rather a do-gooder, I suppose, nothing all that impressive, I'd have to say, but—"

"Royce!" Becky interrupted, furiously, "that's not fair! Neal is . . . is—"

Royce laughed at his sister's discomfiture. "Neal has always been Becky's favorite. Oh come now, Sis, you know that's so. You see him through fond eyes; I'm more realistic."

"For shame, Royce! Neal is every bit as good-looking, as smart . . . and kinder—"

Royce interrupted, " 'Nuff said! You can back off, little sister! Neal truly is," he finished sincerely, "a rock of a man, a solid citizen, and much more agreeable, I guess you'd say, than I am. Satisfied, Sis?"

Red-faced, Becky spluttered, "I didn't mean—"

"We're both committed to making a go of it. I can't tell you," Royce's voice quickened, "how satisfying it is to carve

131

a home from sheer bush! It's not been easy and," his eyes swung to Marlys's, "it won't be easy, probably ever. But as I say, it's tremendously gratifying. It's the life for me—and for Neal."

And for me, Marlys's eyes seemed to say as they turned, full-orbed and speaking, to the man's face.

"It would take a very special kind of woman," Wilda said quietly, "to be willing to share a life like that. I'm not sure I could do it."

"I see it as a challenge!" Marlys, exalted, seemed to see beyond the confines of the dining room to the far horizons. Meg had to admit it heightened her sister's color, brightened her eyes, and turned her, clearly, into a modern-day Joan of Arc.

Even I have trouble not believing her, Meg found herself thinking, adding grudgingly, *maybe she is serious after all.*

There was nothing to do about it anyway; Meg determined to put her own disappointment aside and trusted her sister's motives to be good ones.

Rising from the table, Royce asked Harley, in an aside, "May I speak with you . . . privately, that is?" And Harley took the young man into the small library room to the side of the parlor.

Helping Fanny and Wilda clear the table, Meg and Becky exchanged glances; Marlys was standing, tense, staring out into the garden. At the eventual sound of the opening door she turned, a satisfied smile touching her lips at the expression of relief on Royce's face and the expansive grin on the face of her brother.

It was a foregone conclusion to everyone, and no one was surprised when Marlys took Royce's arm and turned him toward the parlor. Harley nodded significantly to the others and herded them silently toward the back part of the house.

"He's asked for her hand, of course," he murmured when they were out of hearing. "And," grinning, "I couldn't think of a reason to say no. It looks as if we'll be losing one of our boarders, Wilda. Meggie, you plan on sticking around for a while, eh?"

Meg reassured him, and if her tone was hollow no one noticed but Becky.

Becky had made her way home and Meg was reading in her room, trying to concentrate when the door opened, Marlys floated in, closed the door, and leaned on it, her arms flung wide, her eyes closed, her pink mouth smiling.

"You may be the first to wish me happiness!" Marlys said, opening her eyes and seeing Meg's speculative gaze on her. "Oh, come on, Meg, don't be a spoilsport! Or is it a case of sour grapes?"

Doing her best to ignore the cruel thrust, which hurt, nevertheless, Meg merely asked, "And when is the great day to be?"

"Why, that isn't settled," Marlys said lightly, moving from the door to her favorite place—the mirror, "I think blue—the color of my eyes . . ."

"What do you mean, it isn't settled? It has to be during one of the few days left before Royce goes back, doesn't it?"

"Why no, silly! Of course, that's what Royce wants. But I'm not ready. I don't mean I'm not *emotionally* ready. I mean I don't have a proper trousseau. There are ever so many things I need—"

Meg was astonished. "Need? I should think you'd be more interested in weeding out what you already have too much of."

"They're all the wrong things. Besides, it will be so

thrilling to be apart for a while and then see the eagerness on Royce's face when we meet again."

"So Royce and Becky are going back without you. If I were a prospective bridegroom and wanted and needed a wife as much as he seems to, I think I'd be pretty disappointed—"

"Well, naturally! But I managed to get him to see my side of it. Besides," Marlys seemed to have a need to use the word, "this will give him time to do a few of the things around his place that will make it more comfortable for me."

Poor Royce, Meg thought. *I had the idea he was pretty proud of his place and well satisfied with it.*

"Anyway, Royce and Becky will leave next Monday. That will give us over the weekend to make plans. Ooh, Meggie—isn't it exciting? Me, a married woman!" And Marlys whirled and danced around the room until she was dizzy and dropped onto her bed to finally calm herself and say, frowning, "You'd think he would have had a ring ready!"

18

With the coming of a new day, the Lamb family scattered soberly for the implementing of the final phase before leaving Toronto, with its grinding poverty.

Wildrose would have its poverty but not like the stark hopelessness of the urban poor. There would always be food—simple, perhaps, but enough of it and always nutritious. That it would take hard work they knew. But they were already working hard and for small satisfaction.

In fact, Freddy's efforts had been little short of catastrophic. Amanda, trying to summon strength for the day, felt chilled to the very core when she thought how close they had come to losing him. How quickly he might have been whisked off to prison. Prison! It seemed incredible that children should be trundled, willy-nilly, to a life of severe incarceration with such dispatch. John Kelso, a police reporter, kept the public informed of the atrocities the penal system subjected its littlest lawbreakers to. His articles in the Toronto *World* told of children as young as six being sent to prison for theft. What could a six-year-old lift, to warrant that? Perhaps, like Freddy, nothing more serious than a bottle of milk.

It was wrong of Freddy, Amanda knew. But that he had been thrust into such a position filled her with anguish;

whether to be understanding or condemning struggled in the motherly bosom. But it must not happen again! If not an awaiting prison, it could be the orphanage.

But was it a better alternative? When Kelso had looked into the situation, concerned that children were not given protection and care, he was told that children were "too dirty and their language offensive" for consideration.

If the orphanage officials stepped in, it would involve all of them. With fear and trembling Amanda approached the next few days, the last before they could expect to take the train out.

Leaving for work earlier than the others, to allow for the long trip across town from The Ward to the respectable, affluent neighborhood of the Sylvesters, Amanda could waste no time. As always, she pinned on an ancient hat and buttoned up her threadbare gloves and, her hand on the knob, looked back at the six faces turned toward her so seriously and managed a smile.

"Just a few more days, darlings."

"Just a few more days, Mama," they chorused.

"And, Freddy—"

"You don't have to worry, Mama. I promised."

"And, Jake—" Amanda hesitated.

"I remember, Mama. I promised."

Giving a last look at each dear face, Amanda turned and stumbled away, calling up reserves that hadn't been needed before. Would they be enough?

Lev Rosen stepped from his doorway. "Mrs. Lamb. I just want to say . . . well, that Officer Riley—"

"You know, of course, Mr. Rosen. Have known, perhaps?"

Lev Rosen shrugged. "Officer Riley is a kind man,

Ma'am, behind that badge and that bluster."

"Thank God!"

"Of course." The man looked at Amanda's white face closely. "I'm here, if you need me. Just want you to know that you—and the tadpoles up there—you can all count on me."

"Oh, Mr. Rosen, whatever should we have done without you!" Amanda's eyes filled with tears.

"Well, Ma'am," the little scarecrow of a man said, eyes half screwed shut, jutting nose and jaw close to meeting over the near-toothless mouth, "I promised Mr. Lamb—when he settled you all here and left you—that I'd keep an eye out for you."

Her third promise today. It was almost more than Amanda could assimilate. "And you have, you've been a dear, dear friend! We'll soon be gone, Mr. Rosen, but till then—" Amanda hesitated.

Lev Rosen's voice was gentle but resolute. "I'll be here for them."

And the landlord and dealer in used goods watched as the stable hand, the barbershop sweeper, and the newspaper hawker came down the stairs, passed through the door, to another day's work. Only then did he close the door to his lonely room.

Only half aware, sick of body, burdened of heart, Amanda paid her nickel and found a seat on the electric car. Eventually someone tapped her arm and said, "Ain't this your stop?" and she started, murmured a thank-you, and stepped down, moving automatically past the homes of the prosperous and the fortunate. Well-cared-for lawns, beautiful gardens, every house was embellished with rollicking friezes and gingerbread scrolls, with cornices from which grinning gargoyles surveyed the street. Massive doors promised equal magnificence beyond.

Inside, parlors and drawing rooms were crowded with the bric-a-brac that symbolized the era of the '90s. Scarcely an inch but what was adorned, even congested, with cupids and cherubs, carved boxes and japanned trays, enameled clocks and cloisonné vases, wax flowers, and hair flowers. Heavily flocked wallpaper was covered with outrageously ornate frames filled with family portraits and dark landscapes.

And bustling through them, "help," like Amanda, had come from small rooms with bare floors, no plumbing and often only one tap of water for many needs, uncared for children, and, sometimes, rampant vice and wickedness.

Turning in at one gate, Amanda made her way around to the back and the kitchen entrance.

"Morning," the cook greeted her, adding, "Hey, you all right?"

Amanda nodded, laid aside her hat and gloves, and turned to the cellar steps.

"Better keep an eye on her today," the cook said to the girl washing up the breakfast dishes. "She don't look none too good at any time, and she looks worse today."

And so it was that the young "scullery" worker, upon hearing only silence from below, eventually slipped downstairs. White-faced and trembling, she ran breathlessly into the kitchen.

"Something's happened to Mrs. Lamb! Come quick!"

Cook hurried down. "Call the Mrs.!" she commanded.

When Mrs. Sylvester arrived, she and cook between them lifted an inert Amanda from the tub over which she had collapsed, hands hanging uselessly down, wisps of hair floating in the soapy water.

"Is she drownded?" squeaked the frightened little maid, wringing her hands.

"Her *face* wasn't in the water, goose!" gritted cook, as frightened as the girl.

"Lay her here," Mrs. Sylvester directed, and they lowered the limp body onto a pile of laundry. Mrs. Sylvester began feeling for a pulse, and cook knelt down at Amanda's side, rubbing a flaccid hand.

"Quick, girl!" the lady of the house ordered, "go find Geordie—he'll be in the greenhouse—and send him for the doctor! Scoot!"

And the child scooted, located the gardener, and spread the word among a quietly gathering staff.

When the doctor arrived, Amanda had been moved by male members of the staff to a small room off the kitchen. Everyone was ejected except Mrs. Sylvester, and the doctor began his examination, listening to the patient's heart, checking her pulse, lifting her eyelids. Listening, listening, to her chest.

"Hmmm. If she doesn't have consumption, she's very near it," he said, circling the blue-veined wrist with his fingers. "Probably underfed and overworked."

Mrs. Sylvester looked uncomfortable.

"She needs the hospital, of course." And the man of medicine lifted an eyebrow at the woman of wealth and fixed her with a straight look.

"Well, of course . . . of course, we'll take care of her. I don't think her husband is in evidence in her life, for some reason or another."

"Children, no doubt?"

"Yes—we'll get word to them. Doctor, I'll consult with my husband, but I feel we should stand the expense of this. I've tried . . . in my way . . ."

Mrs. Sylvester paused, knowing she had helped Mrs. Lamb far too inadequately, her concern was too careless. Being a good woman at heart, her conscience smote her now.

"Get her to the hospital, Doctor. If there is an . . . an indigent ward . . . if not, of course, we'll see to her care."

When a frightened Jake and Ammie crept to her hospital bedside, Amanda's white hands gripped theirs while she tried to stem the weak tears that ran down her thin face. The tears and fear on the faces of her children served to choke back her own tears and firm her voice as she greeted them.

"We probably won't have long to talk," Amanda whispered when they had quieted. "Jake, do you remember what we talked about? What I prepared you to do, if necessary?"

"I remember, Mama, but I never thought . . . I never thought—"

"I know. The thing is, you must go ahead and get ready to leave. Just as soon as I'm out of here, we'll be on our way. Can you do that? Get Mr. Rosen to help you find some boxes or crates or perhaps a secondhand traveling bag."

"We'll take care of it, Mama."

"The thing I fear," Amanda's hollow eyes were haunted with the thought, "is that the authorities . . . or someone . . . will turn you in, will report that you're there alone—"

"There are children all over the city who are alone! On the streets . . ."

"I know, but there's some kind of movement now, people are aware of the problem—the city officials and the orphanages—and they are making an effort, a special effort at this time. You must be very careful. Try not to let anyone but Mr. Rosen know you are alone."

With many assurances, a few more tears, and sad good-byes, Jake and Ammie left. Amanda, exhausted, closed her eyes and prayed. Never a praying woman, other than a routine grace at mealtimes, Amanda prayed. Not for herself, her faith didn't extend that far, but for her children: "O God, take care of my children! Please, please! Take them to be with their father . . . please . . . please . . ."

19

"La, there they are now!" Miss P said, hearing the sound of a rig in the yard.

"And I'm just fine," Lily said, settling back against the pillows Miss P had tucked around her chair. "Go on with you!" And Lily waved her nurse away. With a book at hand and cup of tea available, Lily had indeed been well cared for. The ankle, though swollen and sore, had been pronounced sprained by Anna Snodgrass.

Happily aflutter with responsibility and being needed, Miss P closed the door behind her and hurried across to her own house. Here two children were scrambling from a buggy, the reins being held in the plump hands of Dovie Ivey, middle-aged bride of neighbor Digby Ivey and sister to Anna Snodgrass and twin to Dulcie.

Love and pride shone in Dovie's face. "Now be good children," she said unnecessarily but enjoying the saying almost as much as the children loved hearing it.

Holly and Neddy Carroll had only recently joined the family of Dovie and Digby or, more correctly, *become* the family of Digby and Dovie. The entire district had rejoiced in the love affair between the middle-aged man, father of one grown boy, and Dovie Snodgrass, long an old maid but quickly and fully embracing her married status. Until, that is, she lost three babies and, time having run out, was tempted to despair. But Dovie's unrelenting persistence in believing an obscure scripture had them all trembling for her faith and had resulted in the surfacing of the orphaned Carroll children, to be loved and adopted by their new parents, to the satisfaction of everyone.

Miss P, while rejoicing with her neighbor, hid her own empty heart and, as was her way, made herself indispensable to Dovie and the children and was very soon known as Aunt Phoebe (Aunt Miss P having been rejected as unsuitable).

Now the children had come to "play" with Aunt Phoebe while Dovie went to the Snodgrass place to visit with her sisters and to check on Shaver, Digby's son, who was helping the "girls" run the homestead since dear Papa's death.

Having checked old Biddy's nest and found the eggs not yet hatched, squealing when Biddy's quick beak pecked the searching fingers, and having climbed the hayloft to play with the baby kittens and each choosing their own favorite, Neddy and Holly and Miss P returned to the house. Now the fun began in earnest.

Miss P had promised that the children should bake pies. With the youngsters trudging at her heels, Miss P went into her pantry, handing ingredients to the waiting hands. Then a trip by all three to the cellar resulted in the assembling of the lard, which Miss P set Neddy to measuring into a teacup while Holly, with another teacup, measured the flour.

"Half as much lard as flour; half as much cold water as lard," Miss P chanted, having learned the directions just that way at her own mother's knee.

Miss P had cut the first rhubarb of the season into bite-sized pieces. Now they were mixed with the proper amount of sugar and flour and arranged in each of the three pies: one for Neddy and Holly to take home, one for Lily and Luther, and the last one for Jacob Lamb.

"We never met Jacob Lamb," Neddy said. "How come he gets a pie?"

"He lives all alone," Miss P began, to be met by sympathetic cries and listening ears. Neddy and Holly had known the sorrow of losing a mother, living with their father alone on the prairie, and struggling to survive when he died.

"But he's not really all alone in the world," Miss P quickly explained, and the children breathed easier. "He has a family in Toronto, back east. There's a girl, Josie, just about your age, Holly. When they come, I'm sure you can be a friend to her."

"She'll just love Wildrose," Holly said knowingly, having found happiness and contentment herself.

The pies assembled, a little more lumpy than usual, perhaps, but "just perfect" to the children, Miss P thrust her arm into the oven and deemed it just right for pies, and they were set inside.

But not before Miss P had taken strips of old sheeting, dampened them, and wound them around the rim of each pie, just as her mother before her had done.

"To keep the juices from running over into the oven," Miss P explained to the questioning children, and they nodded wisely.

Now came a spate of assessing the burning wood in the stove, adjusting the drafts, and checking the clock to begin timing.

"Now," Miss P said mysteriously, "I have a very special treat." And she gathered the children beside her on the sofa and opened a brand-new book, carefully pressing its pages until it lay flat.

"Oh boy, *Black Beauty!*" exclaimed Holly, who could read.

Miss P, thinking of Neddy and Holly and the coming family of Jacob Lamb, had not been able to resist the ad in *The Youth's Companion* and, once again blessing Uncle Roscoe, had gladly sent off the 10 cents in postage stamps in payment, as requested. For it she had received, as promised, the "New Edition, Handsome Eight Color Lithographed Cover," 200-page book, which Neddy and Holly now found so appealing. The *Philadelphia Star*, or so the ad reported, had called *Black Beauty* the "*Uncle Tom's Cabin* of the Horse." The *New York Independent* was quoted as saying, "This book has the fascination of a story, the truthfulness of an essay, and the moral sincerity of a sermon." But, of course, Miss P didn't tell the children this.

She said rather, "*The Philadelphia Ledger*—that's a newspaper in the States—says 'no more useful or entertaining book can be put into the hands of boys and girls.' "

"How come it's in *your* hands, Aunt Phoebe?" Neddy asked, and he received a kiss on the top of his head for his cleverness.

Having established the importance of the treasure they were about to explore, Miss P duly began to read. When the clock indicated the pies were done and the house filled with a luscious aroma, the book was laid aside and the baking lifted anxiously out and set to cool.

"How would you like to have lunch with Lily?" Miss P asked and explained about Lily's twisted ankle. The children enthusiastically agreed. First it meant a trip to Miss P's garden and the picking of the largest lettuce leaves they could find among the tender new growth, washing them in fresh cold water at the well, and laying them carefully on slices of Miss P's homemade bread after they had been

slathered manfully, by small Neddy, with Miss P's homemade mayonnaise.

With Neddy and Holly carrying the tea-towel-topped
basket between them and Miss P hovering over them, they
took the sandwiches, pickles, and jiggling bowl of blanc-
mange pudding to the Boggs's shack, where they were
greeted cheerily by a lonely and frustrated Lily.

Soon the sound of Dovie's rig could be heard and her
voice calling.

"No, I better not get down," she answered Miss P's invitation, "or I'll never get away. There's just too much to visit
about. The most recent news," she happily relayed, "is that
Royce Ferguson has got himself engaged. He and his sister
should be back soon, according to Neal. Now *there's* a
young man, Miss P, that any girl would be happy to have!"
Dovie, so new to the ways of love and marriage, nodded
wisely.

"The new bride isn't coming?"

"Not yet, according to Neal. Well, jump in, children!"

But first the pie must be brought and set in the buggy's
box, then, to the cries of "We'll come next week and you
can read some more to us," they were off, and Miss P
turned to additional satisfactory endeavors.

What a day it had been thus far! She thoroughly anticipated the next hour or two with Jacob Lamb, presenting
him with the cushions she had made for his rocking chairs
and setting the pie, made from the summer's first rhubarb,
on his old but handsome oak sideboard. The elderly uncle
who had lived there had owned a few very fine pieces; the
Lamb family would not be destitute or have any need to feel
they were living in totally primitive conditions when they
arrived, as some newcomers must, arriving with only a
wagonload of goods that they would set up in a quickly

erected shack or cabin if they were lucky or a hillside dugout if they were not.

Luther being away, Miss P harnessed and hitched Old Mag, loaded her offerings for a lone man who was "baching it," put on her hat, and started down the road.

With the peace and natural beauty of the virgin bush flourishing around her, taking on summer's richer, darker green, Miss P was totally unprepared for what she found when she dismounted from the buggy, hallooed vigorously, and, getting no response, pushed open the door and entered, to an obviously empty house.

Well, of course, he didn't know I was coming, Miss P told herself. But his buggy was in the barnyard and both of his horses in the corral. Leaving Old Mag, head lowered, in a somnolent state and perfectly contented, Miss P walked to the barn.

Opening the door, she was startled by the quick beat of threshing hooves; some creature, in a darkened stall, was dancing and quivering and blowing heavily. Throwing the door more widely ajar, Miss P, frowning, approached the excited animal. Now she could see the tossing head, the rolling eyes, the rope stretched taut. Now she could see, underneath the flashing hooves of the stallion, the crumpled body of a man.

Her entrance had alarmed the horse; the closer she stepped, the wilder he became.

"Jacob!" she managed, and the stallion's front feet rose in a frenzy of slashes until the rope pulled tight and he dropped down, one hoof striking the huddled body below.

Knowing she could do nothing, Miss P, trembling like a poplar in the wind, backed out, closed the door on a scene that would never fade from her memory, and ran for her rig.

Never had Old Mag been so startled; never, in recent

years at least, had so much been expected of her.

Her place being closest, Miss P pulled in, praying that Luther would be home. He came from his shack at the sound of her screech.

"It's Jacob Lamb! Oh, Luther, it's terrible! He has a stallion in the barn . . . and he's lying under it! I couldn't get to him! Oh, Luther, what'll we do? You can't possibly get that creature out of there by yourself. Oh, what'll we do?"

"I'll go right away," Luther said. "You go on down the road . . . get whoever's at home along the way and send them on. And . . . get Anna."

Anna Snodgrass! Of course! But could even Anna mend a body broken by those wickedly slashing hooves?

20

If Royce Ferguson had ever had any tentative thoughts of her as a prospective bride, Meg thought sadly, he had put them aside rapidly. And, apparently, happily. In the few days remaining before he left for his homestead, Royce and Marlys spent nearly every minute together.

Marlys glowed, Royce beamed. Meg sighed and determined to be happy for them. Becky's lips tightened, and she said, "I'm just as glad she isn't going when we are. I'll have a much better time. And it'll give me time to feel at home. I'll just get settled, I suppose, and she'll come and take over!" Becky was a bit petulant.

"Well," Meg consoled, "you can live with your other brother, can't you?" And Becky brightened.

"He's ever so much more fun than Royce," she said. "Royce is getting quite—aged."

Meg could only laugh, seeing Royce as the epitome of all things masculine. True, he had seemed a bit . . . Meg hesitated to use the word "stuffy"; "mature" was better. And even that was mellowing under Marlys's gaiety. Would Marlys ever be serious about anything? She flitted through the days and wafted through the evenings, and Meg could understand the charming web she wove around any man of her choice. When all was said and done, Meg grudgingly admitted, Marlys had shown better sense in her final choice than had ever been expected of her.

Finally, the day of their departure, Becky and Royce stopped by on their way to the train for a final good-bye. Marlys and Royce closeted themselves behind parlor doors, and, to the waiting Meg and Becky, the silence was telling. Becky grimaced, "Love!"

Marlys, when the couple emerged, was pink-cheeked and rosy-lipped and trying to appear modest about what had obviously been a fervently demonstrative leave-taking.

"It's time he was on his way," Harley whispered grimly in an aside to a disapproving Wilda.

At the door and at the gate, where they all walked with Becky and Royce to the waiting rig, the engaged couple had exchanged soft and meaningful looks. Then, with a final clasping of hands and a squeeze or two that Meg could hardly interpret, never having tried it, there was nothing left but called "Good-byes." Before they whirled out of sight around a corner, Royce turned and gave one final wave. Marlys, kissing her hand, was drawn roughly back by her outraged brother.

"For heaven's sake, Marlys! Show a little discretion!"

"If you'd ever been in love," said Marlys repressively, "you'd understand." Then, catching sight of Wilda's wrathful face, added, "Oh, sorry!" and slipped past her family to the house.

Upstairs together, Marlys collapsed on her bed, not, as Meg at first supposed, with lonely sobs but with laughter.

"Did you see Wilda's face? Oh, that was rich!"

"You hurt her feelings," Meg said, taken aback at this new thoughtlessness of her sister.

"She's such a stick! You'd think the world was made up of babies and bottles and nappies and naps!"

"What kind of a life do you think you're setting out on?" Meg asked.

"Adventure! Romance! New horizons! Oh, Meg, get that look off your face!"

"I just can't believe you haven't grasped the reality of it, that's all. It's so raw and crude on the frontier, Marlys. There'll be no emporiums, no summer residence to escape the sultry months, no 'at homes.' You'll certainly have no need of those calling cards you just had made up."

Marlys's cards, bearing no address, which was right and proper for a lady, were of medium weight bristol board, engraved with black ink. Carried in an ornamented case, they were presented with great satisfaction, with the appropriate corner turned down to express a specific message. The corners on the left side, top and bottom, meant "felicitations" and "condolences." The right side, "delivered in person" and "to take leave." It was all a puzzle to Meg, but then, she had never been invited to accompany her sister, who had found a rapid entrance into genteel society with its strict etiquette.

Marlys looked a little unsettled at Meg's reminder of the life that awaited her, where a home was utilitarian rather than fashionable, where a wife and mother had a responsibility—not only to her husband and children but to helping provide food for the table, raising it, canning it, even milking it, hoeing and weeding . . . burning her tender skin in a garden . . .

Marlys thought of these things uneasily and turned her thoughts quickly from the demands of a pioneer home, the isolation, the lack of medical care, the anxiety over food supplies, the endless months of cold, the frightening blizzards, the lack of ready cash. It was all so unsettling.

Unwillingly, her thoughts turned to the list of supplies

Royce had assembled and which she had watched unbeliev-
ingly: Roll of barbed wire; 12 feet of stovepipe with one
damper-segment; storm lantern; pitchfork; posthole spade;
milk pail with sieve spout; a barrel of lime (surely that
wasn't going into the whitewash that would grace her
walls!); carton of matches; a keg of nails; five pounds of
Rose tea (*not* Marlys's favorite!); a tethering chain; a box of
copper rivets . . axle grease . . . rope . . .

Marlys shifted uneasily, remembering Royce's household list: table salt; 20 pounds of coarse salt for curing
meat; oil of cloves (for toothache!); several sacks of oatmeal; a gallon of vinegar (used, Royce said, in everything
from pickles to hair care to boiling to destroy odors). Vinegar, he said seriously, must never be kept in a stone crock
or jug; its acid attacked the glazing. "The same with
yeast," he had added.

About this time, in Royce's buying, Marlys had gone for
a breath of fresh air, to clear her whirling head. Thank
goodness for Becky, she found herself thinking with a
shrug, and went back in time to ask what the cheesecloth
was for and be told it served several purposes—as screen to
keep out mosquitoes and flies, to squeeze chokecherries
through when making jelly so the resulting juice would be
clear and not cloud . . .

"My goodness, I'm impressed!" she had said, looking at
Royce with an admiration she didn't feel.

"One learns and learns quickly," Royce had said modestly and added treacle and brimstone. "For Anna
Snodgrass," he had said quickly, seeing Marlys's closed
eyes and hearing her indrawn breath. After that, things had
gone better. She could imagine herself (or better yet,
Becky) putting the nutmeg and salt and cinnamon and
ginger and tapioca on the shelves.

But she had paused when Royce had added chamomile. "Its leaves are good for colic," he had explained, "and where there are babies, there's colic!" Obviously Marlys's dismay showed on her face, for once again Royce added quickly, "For Anna. Anna is our midwife and doctor."

All that and more had been crated and shipped. "Neal will think it's Christmas when it arrives," Royce had said with a grin, once again checking his bride-to-be's expression and adding somewhat apologetically, "Some of this stuff we've never had . . . haven't been able to afford it. Couldn't now, of course. Dad and Mum are buying a lot of this for us, perhaps because we'll be looking after Becky. I should add a couple of really big kettles to the pile . . . ever live through a threshing day, Marlys? No? You'll find that a high point of the year, in Wildrose."

Marlys's eyes glazed. Sometimes, she thought, the man can be unbelievably stupid! And then he turned his silvery gray eyes on her, and she immediately decided that she might indeed find threshing a titillating experience.

"Have you decided when you'll go?" Meg was asking, and Marlys turned from her thoughts, sitting up and adjusting her clothes, her hilarity over.

"Oh, in a month or so."

"One month! Why on earth don't you go with Royce now? Are you sure you're going at all?"

"Why do you keep suggesting I'm not going?" Marlys said angrily. "For one thing, I haven't finished my shopping. For instance," and Marlys stood, strode to the chiffonnier, and dabbed Crab Apple Blossom perfume on her temples, "I'm going to lay in a supply of those Lavender Salts we saw the other day. Aren't they supposed to be enjoyable, while curing headaches?"

"That's what it said on the bottle. If it works, you should

invest in a massive supply. You'll need them on, say, threshing day."

Marlys glanced at her sister sharply. Then, answering calmly said, "I'll make sure I have a satisfactory apron or two, of course. Not those black sateen kind Fanny wears or those gingham frights Wilda wears. I saw," she said thoughtfully, "a Victoria sheer white lawn, with three tucks. I believe I'll just run along and see about it now . . ."

When she was gone, Meg pulled from its hiding place a daintily flowered percale apron she had been secretly hemming as a parting gift for her homestead-bound sister. Tying it around her own waist, she shrugged and went down to help Fanny with the weekly task of rug beating.

"The next chance I get," she told herself fiercely, "I won't let the queen herself do me out of it! Wildrose—or wherever—I'll get there yet!"

21

"Neal will think it's Christmas," was what Royce had predicted. And "Wow! It looks like Christmas!" was what he said.

Because Royce was bringing extensive supplies as well as any niceties his bride might want, Neal had been prepared and had taken the wagon to meet his brother and sister. Becky, he thought, would be the finest piece of "baggage" Royce would bring with him.

The train, for once, was on time. Children bent and put ears to the rails, hearing the hum before hearing the engine, and were drawn back by nervous parents. The gathering crowd could hear it and glimpse its smoke before they could see it, but eventually the bellowing monster charged from the bush.

The coming of the train had been a big moment in the lives of bush people, as it was all across the prairies to the south. Life had stepped up a beat with the advent of the train. Goods only dreamed of before were now part and parcel of their lives. Particularly "parcel." Now, delivered to their own post office, the fascinating catalog brought the city's goods into every backwoods home, with considerable excitement. To some the catalog was the "good book." In Wildrose, the story circulated that when the pastor visited in the Milliken home and asked for the Bible, to read a comforting passage, Vera Milliken had called to her small son, "Tommy, bring the book Mama loves," and Tommy had duly produced the catalog.

But men were captivated too. Weary of overalls, the vast selection of clothes, particularly shirts, was tantalizing. A shirt was no longer just a shirt. "To be thoroughly up-to-date you must wear up-to-date shirts," the catalog affirmed, adding, "We have up-to-date shirts for up-to-date people at up-to-date prices." To prove their point, they offered Men's Fancy Bosom Laundered Shirts, "A princely shirt for princely men"; Men's Ideal Outing Shirts, "Have won the highest praise from men who have long wished and longed for something really comfortable as well as dressy, and strictly up-to-date. Correct dressers will all wear them"; Fat Man's Special (most Wildrose men, however, were lean, whether or not by choice).

Under the grand title "Ten Tons of Shirts" were listed:
Blue Chambray Never-rip Shirt
Men's Black Sateen Overshirt
Buckskin Cloth Overshirt
Moleskin Shirt at 74 cents
A $1.50 Silk Striped Madras Shirt for 98 cents
Men's Soft Negligee Shirts . . . flannel shirts, wool shirts . . . corded front shirts . . . madras cloth . . . cassimere . . . woven French . . .

For people whose local store offered less than the basic needs, the catalog was a glorious supermarket. Aside from a dazzling selection of clothes, furniture, farm paraphernalia, musical instruments, books, jewelry, beauty products, and even food, strange and fascinating items could be had for the ordering, bringing a measure of pleasure to the homestead, however isolated, however backward. Tucked away in the odd corners of the hundreds of pages were items such as mourning handkerchiefs, silk mitts, ostrich tips, lorgnette chains, human hair goods with directions about measuring for bangs, 3" by 13" waves, toupees, goatees, side whiskers, full beards, and switches. When Philomina Stultz was considering the purchase of an egg darner, her small son, Paulie, marveled, "I didn't know you could mend cracked eggs!"

With a calf half-grown and unwilling to give up its mother's milk from the "spigot," so to speak, Joe Harvey ordered Fuller's Calf Weaner. Fastened around the calf's muzzle, it in no way interfered with feeding from the ground, but when its head was raised and it attempted to suck, numerous spiky wires jabbed its mother in the tenderest of spots, sending Daisy bounding, bawling across the meadow. Well worth 17 cents!

With his new specs making it possible, at long last, to study the "wish book" along with the best of them, Hubert Runyon secretly and cunningly ordered Almond Nut Cream, planning to get the laugh on Harry with his wrinkles and crevices unattended to. When, after numerous applications, the lotion was found to be "cooling," all right (Hubert kept it secreted under his pillow upstairs, far from the heater), but in no way kept its promise to "clear the skin from wrinkles, tan, freckles, etc., keeping it soft and white," Hubert's wrath knew no bounds.

Finding the empty bottle and studying the fine print, Harry grunted, "You old codger! Almond Nut Cream, indeed! You need *Hazel* Nut Cream—that's what your face looks like, Hu! Last year's hazelnut!"

Harry refrained from saying more for fear Hubert would discover *his* year's extravagance—a bottle of Old Reliable Hair and Whisker Dye, with its alluring "Any shade of color can be obtained, to a light or dark brown or black in a few hours without doing any injury to it, if simple directions are followed." Longing for light brown again, Harry got coal black, and his secret was out.

"Ah-ha!" Hubert exclaimed, reading the label. "Here's the trouble! The instructions weren't simple *enough!* You should have ordered the *extra* simple, Harry!"

Fortunately the potion was as unreliable in its staying power as in its color, and after enough scrubbings to turn Harry's scalp fiery red, it faded considerably.

More dreaming was done over the catalog than buying, for sure. And when it was outdated, it was relegated to the outhouse.

For Neal and Royce there would be little or no need for the catalog and its treasures, at least for a while. The boxes and crates and barrels Royce had packed were being unloaded at the same time Royce and Becky, tired and somewhat disarrayed, were disembarking. For Royce it had been a better trip than when he left for Toronto; now he had Becky to take charge of their meals. A tiny kitchen at the end of the colonist car, though hot and crowded, was available for simple meal preparation. Their mother had packed a large basket with a few battered utensils and with them Becky had scrambled eggs, fried bacon, and heated soup when cans were pried open by Royce. With what they could buy en route and with Mum's good bread and cookies, they had managed.

Becky, having become used to life in a city of more than 86,000 people, with its accompanying gracious way of life, was ill-prepared, in spite of all her brother had told her, for the rawness of the West. Every time a mug or jug upset on the swaying, bucketing train or a child, worn and fractious, went into an unending wail or frustrated conniption fit, she adjusted her expectations and firmed her determination to be a settler whatever the cost.

"Why," she said as civilization faded into a memory and the vast barrens surrounded them, "even the telegraph poles are makeshift!" And they were, being made often of saplings. Crooked and bent, it made no difference as long as they served the purpose. At least, she comforted herself, there was recourse to the telegraph if quick word from home was needed.

Neal had greeted his sister with enthusiasm. "How you've grown!" he exclaimed, holding her at arm's length finally and admiring her.

"Not you," Becky answered. "You've honed down." And it was true; Neal was no longer Royce's unformed kid brother. Almost as tall, though not as heavy, the gray eyes— not as pale as Royce's, but still startling in his work-darkened face—were even more kind than when he was a younger man. Becky admired his strength as, with ease, he helped load the heavy items they had brought. Yes, Neal was a man, and Becky, who loved him as a lad, added admiration to her affection for him.

Every aspect of the country fascinated her. And Neal was a good guide, pointing out various kinds of bushes, some flowering, others bearing new fruit, the host of flowers along the roadside, the birds that filled the day with song as they plodded along, going "home."

Home, for now, was Royce's place. More than a homesteader's first cabin, Royce as well as Neal at his place just over the dividing line, had built well and substantially. The logs were peeled, squared, and set together closely, with chinking between, and whitewashed.

"When you've seen my place, you've seen Neal's," Royce said. "Although we've fixed them up, inside, somewhat differently."

159

The "room," which substituted for drawing room, parlor, dining room, library, and kitchen, was fully half the building. It was comfortable, though crude in many ways. The other part of the house was divided again, making two rooms, and into one of these Royce put Becky's things.

"You'll come over and eat here, Neal," Becky said firmly, and Neal readily agreed.

"Except for tonight," he said, having made plans. The chicken he had put in the oven before he left was ready, and though Becky was weary, she helped, and they soon had potatoes boiling.

"And here," Neal said, producing a bread pudding, "is dessert. I didn't make it," he added hastily, to be interrupted by his brother.

"Don't tell me—Miss P."

And then, of course, the brothers had to tell Becky about this member of the Wildrose family and others.

"We have a letter for Jacob Lamb," Royce said, remembering his visit with the Lamb family and his quick and final stop there to pick up the letter.

Neal's face was instantly grave. "Jacob Lamb," he said, "is dead."

22

At the breakfast table, Jake had looked around at the pinched, frightened faces of his brothers and sisters and tried to be the adult they needed.

"I'm going to see Mum," he said, "and while I'm gone, not a one of you leaves this room. Understand?"

Four heads nodded; Freddy looked rebellious.

"Freddy, listen to me. Not only is Officer Riley keeping an eye out, now more than ever since you . . . you got into trouble . . . Well, that's what it was," he said, in response to the angry flush on his brother's face, "and that lady that's poking around now—Lev Rosen thinks she's from the Children's Aid Society—we have to watch out for her too."

"What does she want?" Joe quavered.

"Us, that's what." Jake was sorry to add to the children's obvious dismay and fright but felt it was necessary in order to keep them in control at the present time.

"Why's she want us, anyway?"

"She wants to do her duty. And her duty, she thinks, is to gather up all the needy children and take them to the orphanage."

Jake's words had the desired effect. "Orphanage" was a dirty word in The Ward. No good report of it was heard, although he supposed they were prejudiced.

"Mostly," he said, "you stay in here because Mum said."

"Can't I go with you?" Ammie asked.

"You know you can't. Not only because you're needed here," Jake gave Freddy a stern look, "but because you couldn't walk all that way. And I'll have to walk . . . or run . . . to save car fare. We can't spend any more of our money than we have to. There's none coming in. Ammie's job is done—"

Ammie looked down quickly, a flush staining her young face.

"And Freddy dassn't work. Not now. It's just too risky. And I've given notice, as Mum asked me to do before . . . before she got sick."

"Did Mama throw up, Jakie?" Josie asked, still not sure just what had happened to put her mother in the hospital.

"She fainted. And Mrs. Sylvester, trying to be good-hearted, I guess, put her in the hospital. When I come home today I'll be able to tell you more about it. Now—do you all know what you've got to do?"

"Stay in!"

"Be quiet!"

"Be good!"

"Die of boredom!" Freddy growled.

Jake thought hard for a minute about his brothers and sisters and their long day and said, "I'll stop and talk to Mr. Rosen and see if he'll bring you up some books or papers. He has hundreds of them stacked around that place of his."

Freddy brightened.

"You, Ammie, and you, Freddy, can take turns reading to the others. At noon, eat the crackers and cheese I brought home last night, and I'll be back before you know it."

With numerous additional warnings, Jake took his departure. Mr. Rosen agreed to hunt out some good books. *"Jo's Boys,"* he thought might be interesting, *"or Aesop's Fables."*

"And Mr. Rosen," Jake said hesitantly, "that woman—"

"I know the one. I think her name is Agatha Crutcher—I've read about her good works in the paper."

"If she gets to nosing around the building—"

"I'll sidetrack her, don't you worry."

Reassured, Jake took off, alternately running and walking, taking advantage of shortcuts and arriving at the big brick hospital in a little more than an hour.

Amanda looked up at her gangly young son with feverish eyes and reached for his hand with a hand that seemed paper thin. Weak tears spilled over. Jake had rarely seen his mother cry during all their trials and hardships, and it was almost more than he could bear. His own eyes teared up, and he sniffed hard and blinked furiously to keep them from running over.

"Listen, Son," Amanda said in an urgent whisper. "There's been a woman in here talking to me about all of you, asking who's looking after the little ones . . . all kinds of personal things. I told her Mr. Rosen was the adult in charge, and I hope it put her off. I'm afraid she'll report to her office."

"Someone—it could be Mrs. Crutcher herself, I don't know—is snooping around The Ward, too, taking notes, asking questions."

"Not snooping really, Jake. She's trying to help. But we don't need her kind of help! It would be disastrous!"

"What are we going to do, Mama?"

"I've been thinking, Jake, now listen to me . . ."

Quietly Amanda revealed her own helplessness. Mrs. Sylvester, thinking she was doing what was best, had left instructions for Amanda's continued hospitalization and care.

163

"I'm bound to this bed as surely as though I were tied to it." Amanda wept. Nevertheless, she was fortunate. It hadn't been long since even reasonable care was unavailable. Doctors had been in the habit of leaving patients in the hands of anyone who was available. Operations were performed on kitchen tables or in doctor's offices, and hospitals had been used only by those who were desperately ill or poor; the well-to-do would have none of them. Hospitals were places of horror to be avoided.

Now the nursing profession was blooming, along with principles of safe, sterile surgery; mortality rates had dropped dramatically, and there was a new outlook on hospitalization. With care and rest, Amanda had been advised, she would recover. But it would take time.

But Amanda didn't have time. Things were too desperate at home.

"I tried to leave," she told Jake now, "but they have taken my clothes. There's no way—" Tears thickened the weak voice once again.

Jake pressed his mother's hand and urged, "Don't cry, Mama. We'll manage, someway."

Gaining control, Amanda said, "I've thought it all through, Son. You and the children must leave. You must go to be with your father. There you will be fed and loved . . . there you will be safe."

"Go—without you?"

Amanda recognized the near-terror in the boy's voice. "You can do it, Jake. Now listen to me—"

Patiently Amanda advised the boy to take the money, buy the tickets, pack up what they could, get to the station, and go. "Take along some food and some clean clothes."

The task seemed monumental for a boy who had never,

to his memory, been more than 20 miles from the city. But Amanda was adamant.

"You *have to,* Jake. There's no choice, unless you want to be divided up, put in an orphanage . . . you're underage, you'd be taken too. Unless," she said, watching his face, "you ran away. You and Freddy—that's what you'd do, isn't it?"

Jake bowed his head; it was answer enough.

"You can't do that! You and Freddy! You have to be there for the others! Jake—answer me! Promise me!"

With shaking voice Jake promised.

Amanda sank back on her pillow, white and spent. "I'll follow, never fear. Just as soon as they'll let me out. You can write me through Mr. Rosen. Leave a few of my things with him . . . take everything else or sell it. Sell what you can, Jake, and go. Go quickly!"

With many tears Jake said his good-byes.

"Just a minute, young man."

About to enter the door to the tenement where the children awaited him, Jake, hot and sweaty from his run, started visibly. It was *the woman.*

Beneath her heavily feathered hat the narrowed eyes studied the boy, looked around at the street, up at the grimy windows of the above floors.

"Are you all right? You don't look well." Perhaps her concern was real.

"I'm fine."

"Your family? Where are they?"

When Jake hesitated, the woman, Agatha Crutcher of the Children's Aid Society, offered an explanation. "I'm asking for a good reason, young man. Don't be afraid to answer me. Could I talk with your mother, perhaps?" The eyes watched the boy keenly.

"Not now . . . she's not home."

"Your father, then?"

"He's not home, either."

"I have it on good authority—there is no man in your household. Isn't that so?"

Jake swallowed, thinking quickly. Obviously she knew his father was gone. But did she know Amanda was away from her children? Had she received that report yet?

"You are welcome, Ma'am, to talk to my mother . . . when she gets home."

"And when will that be?"

"Could you come back after work hours? Say," Jake thought rapidly of all they had to do, "about eight o'clock this evening?"

"I suppose so," the woman said reluctantly. "You understand, I'm sure, child though you are, that it's a very unhealthy thing, emotionally, for children to be neglected, and that what we are doing is a great help in many otherwise hopeless situations." Perhaps skeptical herself, Agatha Crutcher's speech seemed rehearsed.

"Yes, Ma'am."

"Tell your mother I'm coming, young man. And please, all of you be there!"

It sounded like a command. The tense boy said again, "Yes, Ma'am," and escaped.

With narrowed eyes the woman watched, sighed, and turned her attention to the street and the quickly withdrawing figures of its inhabitants. There was not a child, it seemed, present in The Ward today.

If anyone had been close enough to hear, they might have had more sympathy for the lady and her task when she sighed again and murmured, "Why do they resist help, when they need it so desperately?"

Lev Rosen listened to Jake's quite feverishly imparted account of his visit with his mother, her insistence on their leaving, the closing in of the Society. Mr. Rosen, his eyes thoughtful, nodded from time to time, interjected a question or two, and, when Jake was through, spoke briskly.

"Your mother is right, my boy. They'd take you all away and divide you up, and just how you'd ever all get back together is a question. Besides, it'll give your mother peace of mind to know you are out of here and with your father."

"But," the boy sounded desperate, "just how do we go about it? And so quickly?"

"You have the money, I understand?"

"Yes. We've been saving . . . for, well, ever since Papa left." No need to mention the scrimping, the deprivations, the lack the little family had endured; Lev Rosen had seen it all. And helped when he could.

In the apartment behind him and in the basement of his building, Lev Rosen, dealer in used goods, had stored clothing of all kinds. Now he said, "I'll bring up some bags and some boxes. Get Ammie to sorting and packing; Freddy can help her. And you get your money together and get to the railway station and buy the tickets. You know where you're going—?"

"Meridian, Saskatchewan Territory."

"Buy the tickets. Tell them . . . tell them," Lev Rosen said cunningly, "that there's one adult—your mother—four children, and one baby."

"But Mum isn't going, and there's six of us—not five."

"But they need to think your Mum is going in case Mrs. Busybody is nosing around! And don't worry—Mum will get on the train. Oh, not Amanda . . . Ammie."

"Ammie!"

"If you mean to get out of here," Lev Rosen said firmly, "there has to be an adult in the group, simply because the Society is suspicious, with its nose to the scent, so to speak."

"I—I don't understand . . . about an adult, I mean."

"You go get your money, Jake, and take care of the tickets, and leave the rest to me."

"Thank you, Mr. Rosen," the boy said, needing to act like a man and so unsure.

And so it was that when Jake returned, the children were dressed, Ammie in clothing that Mr. Rosen had dredged from his bales of used items. Mr. Rosen had delicately suggested a certain amount of padding for the somewhat outdated but clean and suitable outfit Ammie wore. Not a great deal shorter than her mother, her height would be no problem. Her long hair was fastened on top of her head and fluffed becomingly over her cheeks, and when the wide hat with its foliage, roses, and ribbons was pinned on, the pleated chiffon around the brim helped conceal the face below, particularly when Ammie tipped her head toward anyone who might be looking. Fastened with impromptu haste around the brim was a thick veil; Ammie, with practice, could quickly draw this down and fasten it under her chin.

At Mr. Rosen's prompting, Ammie practiced a sedate walk. "Try to *bustle*," Mr. Rosen suggested, and Ammie swayed, and leaned on the long, slim umbrella Mr. Rosen added to her costume. With a traveling bag of necessities over her arm, even the children were wide-eyed and impressed. Ammie was committed to the need for a disguise and played her role well.

Mr. Rosen looked at his watch. "The dray will be here any minute," he said. "We'll all get on the cars and go straight to the station. You'll be out of here long before dark and when that do-gooder comes, the apartment will be empty."

Mr. Rosen, an eye always out for a sharp bargain, was not reluctant to accept, in return for his help and his contributions, the Lamb family household goods. And, having made the arrangement, Jake felt better about their friend's charity, though willingly offered. What would they have done without him!

One more thing Mr. Rosen promised. Waving to the apprehensive faces peering down at him on the platform, he called, "I'll go see—" About to say "your mother," he saw the well-dressed, scurrying form of Mrs. Crutcher coming toward him with handkerchief waving and steps quickening, and changed it to "Amanda."

"Good-bye, children! Good-bye, Mrs. Lamb!" Innocently, craftily, the old man repeated the farewell until the train and the little family were out of sight.

Then the hand wavered, and the cracked voice whispered, "God go with you, little Lambs!"

23

With the beautiful matched team of bays eager to be gone, and the handsome carriage with its load of young people chattering gaily, Marlys tore open the letter from Royce, scanned it briefly, tossed it aside, and picked up her gloves.

"Coming," she caroled to the dashing young man in the hallway.

About to leave the room to join the outing, Marlys flung crossly at her sister, "Oh, for goodness' sake, don't look like such a prune! I'm simply dying of boredom! As for that letter," she added casually, "do answer it for me, there's a dear. You know what to say. Only," she giggled, "say it with a little more drama . . . leave him, er, *throbbing* with feelings!" And Marlys ran out to join the man who had been much in evidence the last few weeks. Without a ring on her finger to disclose her soon-to-be married status, Marlys was free to resume her social engagements with as much liberty as ever. More so, the family thought, but when they criticized, she had a ready answer.

"Call it a last fling! I'll be an old married lady soon enough. Royce wouldn't mind."

But Meg wasn't all that sure. Neither, apparently, was Harley. The guardian of his sisters, and with Wilda's example, he was uneasy about Marlys's coquettishness. "It's not fitting!" he remonstrated and more than once.

"That new fellow—what's his name? Casper Bigelow? He's entirely too interested. Does he know you're leaving Toronto soon? In fact, two weeks from today, isn't it?"

But Marlys just laughed. And when Harley threatened to tell the apparently enamored newcomer of his sister's coming marriage, a dangerous glint had appeared in Marlys's blue eyes. "Don't do it, Harley. Don't you say anything! I'll handle it."

Harley, mollified, believed her.

Now, with the laughter floating back from the departing carriage, Meg slowly picked up Royce's most recent letter.

"Dearest Marlys," she read. "Though I've just been gone from you for a few weeks, it seems forever. Your letters, though appreciated, are a very poor substitute for your own dear self! Our time together was too short!

"Becky has the place looking very nice—a task that will be yours, my love, hereafter. What a delight it will be to have you share in my work, my plans, my future! I am so eager to take you over the homestead, show you the clearings I have made (not without much hewing and grubbing!), the garden I have put in for you, the pin cherries that will be ripening . . . you will love it all, as I do . . ."

Meg half-groaned. "I hope so. Oh, I hope so," she murmured, having easily transported herself to that far-off, dreamed-of homestead. Royce's pleasure in it and what he had accomplished came through palpably in his letters; her response was spontaneous.

Reading on, Meg could almost smell the fragrance of the wild roses. For yes, Royce said they would be in full bloom when Marlys arrived.

"You can carry a bouquet of them at our wedding, if you wish," the letter continued.

171

"And now, my dear Marlys, I only need have you confirm the date and time of your arrival. It is much anticipated, I assure you. Once having set my heart on you, I'm eager to be married. I'll have things ready, either for a wedding when you get here or, if you wish, the next day. Becky is here, of course, and is a perfectly suitable chaperon should you decide to wait.

"I look forward to hearing from you, and I send assurances of my love and devotion. Yours forever, Royce."

"Answer it," Marlys had said. That casually, she had said it, that carelessly.

Slowly Meg sat down at the desk. Thoughtfully she drew a piece of stationery toward her.

"My dear Royce," she wrote. Thinking of him, lost in the charm of Wildrose, the thoughts flowed easily and swiftly. She wrote as though inspired.

"Dear Royce: It was glorious [Meg paused over the word, but remembering Marlys's injunction to be dramatic, used it] to hear from you. It's not the same without you, and I yearn to come and be with you."

Meg had an uncomfortable moment when she wondered if she were writing for Marlys or herself. Stiffening her courage, she wrote on.

"I could almost smell the fragrance of the roses and see the cattle in the meadow! I can almost picture the house and imagine our happiness in it."

Meg caught herself in time to keep from sending love to Becky. What a giveaway that would be!

"I am filling in the time with [again Meg paused, wondering how to describe Marlys's diversions and the satisfaction they provided for her restless, pleasure-loving spirit] shopping for last-minute things I may need and spending meaningful [a good safe word; Meg had to admire it] contacts with friends here that I shall not see again or at least for a long time after I leave. I count giving them up a small sacrifice in comparison to what I shall be gaining in choosing you, my dear Royce, and a life in Wildrose.

"As to my proposed schedule, I have allowed myself two more weeks here and have my plans made to leave then."

Marlys's date of departure had been openly discussed, and now Meg parlayed that specific information to Royce.

"You asked whether we should be married when I arrive or later. We have been apart enough! Let us be married as soon as I get there. And, Royce, remember that a groom should not see his bride until the moment of the wedding— it has to do with good luck—I will leave the train in my wedding finery, and I suggest that you have your brother meet me and take me to the altar! That way you shall be as eager as I!

"Until that wonderful moment, I remain, your loving bride-to-be, M."

Addressing the envelope, Meg supposed wryly that a secondhand romance was better than none. Placing the letter in the hand of the postman she sighed, "There! Signed, sealed, and practically delivered. And that's the end of that."

As restless now, in her way, as her sister, Meg finally settled down to write to Becky but found it hard going; there seemed so little of any consequence to say. It was all old news to Becky and humdrum. Humdrum in the extreme and tedious in comparison to what Becky was experiencing. Life, to Meg, was tasteless, meaningless. Worse, it was frustrating. Meg grappled with the restrictions placed on her simply because *she was a woman.* To be so bound by convention!

"It's not fair!" she muttered angrily and threw down her

pen, unaware of the ink blots mingling on the stationery with the tears that now flowed freely.

Hunched miserably over the desk, letting her despair and disappointment have their way and facing the prospect of similar meaningless days ahead for as long as she could imagine, Meg failed to hear the approach of the rig. The closing of the front door jolted her into an awareness of her appearance. Swiping at her wet cheeks with the flat of her hand and desperately seeking a handkerchief to eliminate any signs of her state of mind, Meg was an inadvertent listener to the conversation in the parlor adjoining the small den where she sat.

"The ride was all too short," Casper Bigelow was murmuring with the inflection Meg had come to recognize throughout her sister's string of triumphs. There were guidelines to the game: the approach, the tentative suggestions, the hints, the double meanings proceeding to the bold glance, the discreet but tantalizing physical contact . . .

Horrified that she would be discovered, *weeping,* Meg breathed shallowly and moved not so much as a muscle, feeling distinctly uncomfortable.

Marlys murmured something, and Casper's voice brightened. "A capital idea! Tonight! And this time—just the two of us. Now," he murmured intimately, "that will keep me impatient all day! But you . . ." indistinct, muffled, as though with pent feelings, "are worth waiting for."

More murmurs, certain rustlings, silences more speaking than words.

"Until tonight," the somewhat dazed masculine voice was saying, and soon the front door closed and Marlys's steps approached the den door.

"Had a ringside seat, didn't you?" she asked lightly while Meg wondered what had given her away.

Meg merely shrugged. Reproaches were meaningless where Marlys was concerned.

"Writing my answer to Royce?" Marlys asked, glancing down at the desktop. "Making rather a mess of it, aren't you?"

"This is to Becky," Meg said. "The one to Royce is long gone."

"And what did I say?" Marlys was unbuttoning her gloves and stripping them off.

"Not much. I guess the only important thing was to give him the date you are leaving."

Marlys stopped working with her gloves abruptly. "You what?"

"It's no secret, is it? You told us all you'd be leaving—"

"Well, you outrageous blab!"

Meg blinked.

"Where is it? Where's the letter?" Marlys looked around wildly.

"Gone."

"You *mailed* it?"

"It's not like that's the first time I've ever written a letter for you, Marlys!" Meg said somewhat defensively. "And that *is* the date you're leaving, isn't it?"

"You idiot! You noodle!" Marlys's anger grew to frenzy.

"What's going on here?" It was Wilda. Hearing the commotion she had come running from the kitchen. "Marlys . . . Meg! What's wrong?"

"This . . . this addlepated—" Words failed the furious Marlys. Meg drew back in some alarm from the heated countenance of her irate sister. Used to the extravagances of her emotions and her expressions, still this seemed too much to take with equilibrium. Certainly Wilda was not about to stand for it.

"Hush, Marlys! For shame, talking to your sister that way!"

"Do you know what she has done?" Marlys shrieked. "She's written to Royce—"

"You told me to!" Meg inserted defensively.

"She told him I'm actually leaving here! She even went so far as to fix the date!"

"But," Wilda soothed, "it was no secret, Marlys. And if you asked her to write for you—"

" 'Just stir his blood a little,' I said! Nothing more!"

"But he needs to know the date . . . he's counting on—"

Marlys kept interrupting. "Then he's got a big surprise coming! I have no intention of going . . . never did have!"

Now both Wilda and Meg were truly astonished. "But you told him—" Wilda began.

"You *promised*—" Meg reminded her, forgetting for the moment that promises never had meant all that much to her sister.

"You're both such dolts!" Marlys cried scathingly. "Can you possibly believe I ever meant to go to that backwoods hole? Me—*milking a cow? Churning? Wearing homemade dresses? Knitting socks?*" She made them sound like dirty words.

"But, Marlys," Wilda broke in helplessly, "what are you going to tell that young man? *How* are you going to tell him?"

"How? Miss Busybody can tell him!"

Marlys stalked from the room, leaving Meg and Wilda to look at each other with blank faces.

"Is she serious?" Wilda, not knowing Marlys as well as Meg did, voiced the question.

Meg, knowing her very well indeed, looked thoughtful.

24

The immigrant train ground its way across interminable spaces, "slow as molasses," one impatient man had said, and jumped off, running alongside until winded, to prove his point. But slowly, joltingly, it made its way westward.

Jake had thought he would never sleep. At times he had held grimly to the sides of the curvetting bunk as the train swayed its way over rails hastily laid in the first place and buckled since by wind and weather. Grimly he acted as a barricade for his two small brothers. In the lower bunk Ammie did the same as the three girls huddled there in weariness and worry. Weary because of the unspeakable difficulties of such a trip, worry because they were never certain the long arm of the Society would not find them and bring them back.

The car was crowded; they were fortunate to have bunks. Although the trickle of immigrants had been slow, it was steadily increasing as the lure of free land drew men like a magnet. Many, like the Lambs, came from Ontario, where they had eked a scanty living in lumber camps or from "stump meadows"—forested land that had to be cut and the stumps pulled, blasted, or burnt before a crop could be planted. The thought of 160 acres of free land on the western prairies, where, except in meandering coulees, not a tree grew, was irresistible. And all for a $10.00 filing fee.

Other families, like the Lambs, were coming to join husbands and fathers who had preceded them, filing for their homestead, building a soddy (before it was over, 10,000 of them would appear on the prairies), and breaking land. This was virgin soil, so rich, they claimed, that it would never need fertilizer. The top three inches of prairie sod was a tight mix of grasses, buffalo willow, yellow bean, and the ubiquitous dwarf rose. It was too tough, at first, to grow wheat, and so flax was the first two crops the homesteader raised after the plow bit in, turning over the rich soil that had never known the feel of steel.

Ammie, accustomed though she was to poverty, was appalled by the miserable soddies they passed occasionally as the train reached the prairies. She knew, of course, that it meant immediate shelter and, for many, was made of the only material available to them—turves from their own soil.

"See," one knowledgeable man pointed out as they passed two tents almost lost in the vast panorama of grass and the man nearby turning over the soil. "That man is getting potatoes in right away," the informant continued, "and then he'll use his own sod to build a house, if you can call it a house. He'll put up a framework of poles and lay the sod around it. The walls will be mighty thick and will keep out the cold all right. But it may drip water in a rain storm, will have a dirt floor, and will be full of fleas. If he's lucky, he will have a glass window in it."

"Our house," Ammie explained, "is in the bush, and it's made of logs."

"You're lucky," the man said. "And you'll have wood to burn rather than grass or, er, whatever else may be available." The speaker was obviously reluctant to use the word *dung* in a lady's presence, and so left Ammie in the dark as to his meaning. "But bush farmers have a terrible job, clearing all that growth before ever any plowing can be done.

"One bad thing about a soddy—it doesn't conform to the requirements of the Homestead Act, that a house worth $300 be built and occupied before title can be obtained."

And so with more sympathy than she had felt previously, Ammie mingled with the immigrants, patiently waiting her turn in the small crowded "kitchen" to prepare meals for her family. Although she usually discarded the hat and veil, the padding remained, and many a puzzled stranger pondered on the matronly female with the big family and the young, unlined face. But they were a motley crew—foreigners who spoke not a word of English, remittance men from the old country whose families were happy to pay them to stay away from the trouble they had caused at home, women answering marriage proposals that had been made by correspondence, and more than one girl of 15 who was a bride. And all—all—with a dream and the gumption to embark on its fulfillment.

Finally there came a day when the blowing seas of grass were interspersed with bushes, then trees, and finally the train was embraced by growth so dense that it was known as "the bush country." Here trees were not as massive as further north, but they were intertwined with willows and berries and nuts until the resulting growth was intimidating to some people and daunting to men who must grub-hoe and chop their fields from it.

When Meridian was announced by the conductor, Jake and Ammie, almost senseless with weariness and yet atremble with anticipation, gathered their brood and their belongings and prepared to disembark. Plumping up her padding and pinning the hat and veil on for what she trusted was the last time, Ammie knew she would never fool her father, who would remember his wife as being slim and totally unlike the lumpish female who would greet him. Soon she could discard the impersonation, safe under her father's protection.

"I'll yank this old veil aside," she said, "and say 'Boo!' Won't Papa be surprised? He remembers me as being about 11 years old."

At last, they all agreed with relief, they would be beyond the threat of the Society and the division of the family.

Standing on the platform with their goods bulked around them, the first thing Ammie did was to take deep breaths, drawing great gulps of air into her padded chest.

"It smells . . . it smells good!" she exclaimed and soon had the entire family clearing their lungs of the train's smoke and the heavy body odors of too many people too long unwashed in too intimate contact.

Their flight from Toronto had meant that no word was sent ahead, and so it was not expected that their father would be there to meet them. In comparison to their earlier problems, it was the smallest concern. They were here! They were safe!

"Excuse me," Jake said, approaching a man who appeared to be in charge of some loading and unloading.

"Yes, son, how can I help you?"

"We need . . . my family and I . . . to get to Wildrose. You know the area—?"

"Well, of course," the man said with a smile. "Wildrose is a district a few miles thataway." And he pointed north and east, to a wall of green.

"Someone expecting you?" the man asked, glancing at

the bunched family watching and waiting down the platform.

"I'm afraid not. You see, we didn't have time, that is, we didn't write ahead to let our father know we were coming."

"Your father?" the station master's eyes narrowed.

"Yes, sir. Jacob Lamb. Would you happen to know him?"

Even to Jake, child though he was and weary past reason, the silence that fell was telling. On top of this, the man shifted, opened his mouth, closed it, looked around as if seeking assistance or perhaps escape.

Rudy Bannister's frantic gaze fell on Gerald Victor, pastor of the Wildrose church. "Excuse me a minute," he said with what seemed like great relief.

Jake, puzzled, watched while his new acquaintance went to the other man, a man who was loading something into a buggy. They talked and the new man turned and looked at Jake and his sisters and brothers.

"Jake," Ammie spoke at Jake's shoulder, "is something wrong?"

"I think they're trying to see about getting us a ride out to Wildrose." Jake sounded more positive than he felt. Was it possible their name and their situation were known to the people here? Had the Society learned of their destination, and were they even now waiting to apprehend them and force them, willy-nilly, to Toronto and into their custody?

If they could get to Papa, they would be safe. But it was with a heavily beating heart Jake watched the approach of the second man, the first man in tow. Automatically he pushed Ammie behind him. "Go back to the children," he said in a low but commanding voice. Ammie, alarmed, did as he asked.

"I'm Gerald Victor," the kind-faced, gray-headed man

said, and Jake automatically extended his hand. "And you are—?"

"Jacob . . . Jake Lamb, sir."

"Well, Jake," the man continued, "I'm the pastor of the church in Wildrose and though your father wasn't well known to me, still I knew him. A fine man."

Knew him? The man's use of the past tense did not escape the younger man . . . boy, for that's all he was.

"Is my father all right, sir?" he asked, heart thudding and eyes apprehensive.

Ammie, watching beside the children, saw the man put an arm around Jake's shoulders, saw her brother's form crumple, saw his head fall, noticed his stagger.

"It was one of the worst moments of my life," the pastor was to say later to Ellie, his wife. And that was saying something for a man who had sat at the bedsides of parishioners slowly dying without anything to ease their agony; had held in his arms the crushed and broken body of a child who had fallen from a hay mow onto a pitchfork below; who had helped bury three children in the same family, all victims of the dreaded diphtheria.

"There he stood, hardly full grown and probably never had to shave in his life, yet acting like the man of the family. It was he who took the news of his father's death back to the family. In fact, he insisted on it . . . wouldn't let me, though I felt like I should offer what comfort I could to that little mother. What a blow, Ellie! To come all this way only to be told your father and husband is dead! Dead and buried! Obviously the news hadn't reached them, though I understand Miss P wrote. It was she who found Jacob, you know, and she has felt a sort of responsibility, hunting out the family's address, writing, seeing that Luther Boggs took care of the horses, milked the cow, fed the chickens, and so on."

"Did you never get to express your sorrow to Mrs. Lamb, Gerry?"

"No, the young man told her . . . them. They just stood grouped there, shocked, I guess, and wordless. There was no other choice than to arrange for them to go on out to the homestead, though what they'll do from now on, I don't know. Perhaps sell and go on back. It's another bush tragedy, and we've had our share and more."

"Poor, poor woman! We'll all need to do what we can. But I know Miss P will be on the job, and she'll keep us informed. How *did* they get to the Lamb place, Gerry. You had only the buggy . . ."

"Rudy Bannister arranged it. Got Kip Carter to take his wagon, load them all in it, along with their stuff, and head out."

"He's not a very good choice, Gerry! Poor, simple man can hardly hold a meaningful conversation."

"That's true, but sometimes silence is better than a lot of talk. Kip will get them there, unload their things, and do what he can to help. I stopped and told Miss P, and the word will get around. I'll go over tomorrow."

Jolting along in the spring wagon, the Lamb family, as though frozen, missed the glory of the bush at its best—birds flashing around and filling the world with cheer, flowers nodding along the roadside, neighbors pausing in their work to wave, and new fields greening between uncut stands of virgin bush. And all pervaded with the unforgettable fragrances of the parkland.

"Mrs. Lamb," the pastor said worriedly to his wife, "is too small to have this burden thrust on her. Poor thing—all those children looking to her for simply everything. She'll have to come up with a meal once they get to the homestead, make up beds . . . face tomorrow . . ."

"Miss P will be on the job, Gerry. She's probably thinking of all that and making plans to help. Mrs. Lamb will have a friend in Miss P."

In the wagon with the silent Kip, their faces blank with their inability to grasp or understand this latest blow, the Lamb family huddled in shock, Jake's thin arms around Joe and Josie, Ammie rocking the big-eyed Kerry, until Freddy forgot his manly stance and he, too, crept to his older sister, to be drawn into the circle of her other arm.

"Ammie," Jake finally roused himself to say in a low but meaningful voice to his sister, "leave that veil in place! No one, no one at all, must know we're alone."

25

"This is the day!" Royce sang out, and "This is the day," his brother Neal agreed.

"This is the day," Becky muttered, with only Neal to hear.

Never having met the intended bride, Neal could form no personal opinion. But that his sister, Becky, was less than enthusiastic, he knew, had known from the day they arrived and Royce had broken the news to the brother who had stayed at home while he went off "bride hunting."

"So," Neal had said, "you had some success. Tell me about her."

Royce had proceeded to do so, in glowing terms; Marlys was so beautiful, so exciting, so full of life, and so committed to a life in the Territories.

"Don't believe it!" Becky had said as soon as Royce was out of hearing. "Beautiful enough, I guess, and exciting, if you like jibes made at the expense of other people. But interested in a homestead? It's a sham, Neal! She's clever enough to pull it off, especially if you're as smitten as Royce seems to be. I don't look forward," she said with some indignation, "to being her lackey. She'll order me around, I know. Or try!"

"It's that bad?" Neal had asked, amused at his little sister's vexation. There was no flippancy in Becky's remark, however. Neal said, "Surely he gave the decision serious consideration."

"How much consideration can you give in a few days? No, he made up his mind, and he went after her. Come to think of it, she went after him!"

"Surely he prayed about it," Neal said thoughtfully, half convinced by his sister's adamant opinion.

"Pray? Royce isn't you, Neal. I think his prayer, if he made one, was 'Lord, bless this selection I've made.'"

"We could pray about it . . . for him," Neal offered. Becky, though reluctant, finally bowed her head when her brother brought this important matter to the Lord. "Father, if this isn't right—for Royce, for Marlys—even now keep them from making a mistake. We all live so closely entwined, it's vital that we all recognize Your will and be happy about it. Let Becky and me see Your hand and Your will in this important step our brother is about to take, so that we may be happy for him."

At the amen Becky sniffed, and Neal wasn't a bit sure she had changed her opinion that this marriage was all wrong. "Miserable" was the word she had used, "a miserable arrangement."

When the time came to leave for Meridian, Royce had made sure the buggy was spic and span and the horse groomed. Marlys should have no call to be embarrassed about her transportation. The house—to Royce's proud eyes it was all that could be expected for the brief time he had been in Wildrose. That it fell far short of Marlys's Toronto home he knew. His hope was that his bride would see it with eyes of love, as he did. So much of himself had gone into its building. So much of Becky had gone into its furbishing and arranging. Perhaps grudgingly, Becky had their first supper prepared, with baking done and waiting on the sideboard, a chicken in the oven.

"You'll know her," Royce said confidently to his brother. "You can't miss her, even if a million others should suddenly descend on Meridian. She's . . . queenly!

"Try and get all her luggage in the rig, Neal, but if not, assure her I'll go for it soon. And now—off you go, you lucky dog! And fall in love with her—just a little!"

Neal dashed away for Meridian and the train. Royce and Becky very shortly went to the parsonage, Becky taking along massive bunches of flowers. Ellie had promised to make a fruitcake and set out her best china cups and saucers.

Marlys would arrive, as mentioned in her last letter, in her wedding dress. Royce, knowing her as he did, fondly imagined how it would be—Marlys preempting the ladies' room, the other travelers gladly giving place to the bride-to-be, perhaps adoring her. Weddings were of universal interest.

Waiting on the platform for Marlys, as arranged, Neal brushed the dust of the road from the new suit Royce had chosen for him and tipped his derby jauntily onto the back of his dark head. Darker in complexion and hair than his brother Royce, more boyish and more slender in build, he drew admiring glances from several young ladies who had gathered, as was the custom, to see the arrival of the train. Mostly no one alighted for Meridian, but it was common knowledge that today Royce Ferguson's "intended" would arrive. In their backwoods isolation, it was enough to bring the curious to the store for supplies and to casually linger around for the train and the incoming bride. And some of those eyes lingered with appreciation on the groom's brother.

Aware of the glances, Neal admitted ruefully that had Royce been with him, his brother would have had the attention. There was something commanding about Royce, and when he turned the full power of those silvery eyes on any female, he had made a conquest whether he had meant to or not. Neal, eyes gray but not startling so, pleasant but natural and unaffected, realized he was not the heartthrob his older brother was and settled for it without rancor or jealousy. He was a man content to be what he was, satisfied with the way the good Lord had formed him.

When the train grated to a steam-punctuated stop, Neal, stepping back behind curious onlookers, watched the lone female descend.

As promised, she was faultlessly gowned, managing to look as though she had stepped from a band box. Her suit, of excellent quality, fit her slender form superbly. The sleeves, he was gratified to see, were a modified version of the vast leg-o-mutton that widened many female forms past any naturalness. The high collar of the snowy waist seemed to hold her graceful little head at an imperious angle, and the hat, more modest than he expected, was carried like a crown on heavy, golden-brown, piled hair.

As the young woman's eyes searched the group, he could see they were wide-spaced under brows as golden as her hair. Her voice, when she spoke, was the only clue to any tenseness. It shook a little as she asked Rudy Bannister, "Mr. Neal Ferguson—is he here?"

All eyes turned toward Neal. Giving himself a mental shake he stepped forward.

"Miss Shaw?" he asked, removing his hat and bowing a little.

"Yes. And you are Neal."

The new arrival extended a gloved hand, which Neal

took gently in his, raising his head and taking the opportunity to look frankly into the eyes just as frankly studying him.

"You look . . . look like your brother," she said, and again he detected an underlying nervousness. Very natural, he knew, and he felt an unexpected surge of protectiveness toward her. *Falling into her trap,* he acknowledged wryly, wondering what Becky would say and wondering at himself, that he would so promptly fall under her spell.

For what had she done to enthrall him? She was innocent of any overt coyness or pretense. In fact, it was her very naturalness that impressed him.

What a frightful turn of events! Love at first sight—was it possible? And to the girl who had pledged herself to his own brother. Neal, for the longest moment of his life—looked into the eyes raised to his and gave his heart to a girl totally unknown to him, along with a pledge never to reveal it.

Drawing a deep breath Neal turned the girl toward the buggy. "I'll do my best to get everything in," he said, helping her up, finding the touch, though proper, to be sweet.

Neal turned, with a groan, to the luggage, surprised that it was no more than what was reasonable. A sensible woman, as well as fascinating! Giving the watching group a nod and what he feared was a pretense of a smile, he stepped up into the rig and took his place by everything that seemed lovely and feminine and knew it to be pledged to his brother.

"I'm sure you're tired," he managed, clucking to the horse and turning toward the break in the bush that meant the road to Wildrose.

"A bit," she confessed. "Is . . . is the wedding set for . . . for today?"

"That's what you said, in your letter," Neal answered with some surprise. *Marlys with cold feet?*

"Of course! It seems pointless to wait!"

Though silence fell between them, it was a natural silence. She seemed absorbed with the scenery, and Neal had to admit it was worth the attention.

"I wasn't prepared," she murmured. "Nothing Royce said began to describe it."

"You either love the bush or hate it," Neal said. "There are people who can't wait to escape . . . find it too claustrophobic . . are totally intimidated by it. And, of course, it's a bear to tackle when it comes to clearing one's land." Ruefully he held up a callused hand. "An axe and a grub hoe for making land, a pitchfork for making hay, a shovel for digging a well . . ."

Her laugh rivaled the birds' for loveliness.

"Now here's a place," Neal said, pointing to what appeared to be a half-finished dwelling gouged into the side of a small hill, "that has been abandoned. Poor fellow had no money and, worst of all, no skills. Probably worked in a mill or something and was at a total loss when it came to grubbing out trees and building a home. Someone else will come along and be glad to have it and will make a go of it." Slanting the bride-to-be a serious look, he added, "So much of it depends on the wife; she can make or break the entire process. The real heroes of the west, Miss Shaw, are the women."

"How have you managed without one?" Her question, though bantering, was serious.

"I've had my brother. We've lived together, worked together, built together, shared all the work. And now, of course, we have Becky. What a blessing she is! And you know—she just loves it! I'd say she is a born pioneer, young though she is. Now, of course, I'll lose my housemate,

Royce. But," he added quickly, "I'm happy for him. And thank goodness for Becky! She'll move into my house."

"Until you find a wife of your own." The gaze from her eyes was straightforward as they looked into his.

"That'll be awhile, I expect. But the good Lord will have someone—the right one—for me, so I'm content to wait until she comes along."

"You believe that?" was the slow and thoughtful question.

"Absolutely! There's a scripture, you see, that is the key to the way I approach this . . . and everything else. 'In all thy ways acknowledge him, and he shall direct thy paths.' "

"I'm familiar with it, of course. I guess I just never have thought to apply it specifically. In general, I suppose."

"But it's specifically we need Him! 'Shall I move to the Northwest Territories?' for instance. 'Who is the right wife for me?' See?"

"Yes, of course." The white teeth bit the pink lip and again Neal sensed the tenseness of his passenger. The gloves were clasped tightly, and the shoulders were stiff.

Neal thought it time to change the subject to something more diverting than whether or not one had prayed over a forthcoming marriage.

"Your outfit," he said, "is very attractive. Very suitable for a bush wedding, I must admit. Ostentation simply doesn't fit here."

The girl, as though in a dream, answered vaguely, "I thought it would be something I could get a lot of wear out of. The wedding," she said abruptly, "you say it's . . . it's all set up?"

"Yes," Neal answered patiently. "You mentioned that in your last letter—"

"Of course."

"No doubt you are as eager as Royce. He's not been himself, I can tell you that!" Neal's voice was amused. Still his companion showed no sign of relaxing. "But," he reassured her, "he's one happy fella! He was really set at ease by that final letter; he'd been sort of uneasy until he got that one. Becky and I, Miss Shaw, appreciated what it meant to him, and we've seen him settle down happily, certain he's made a good decision. Come now, let's see you feeling just as sure and just as happy." Neal smiled teasingly at the nervous bride and was rewarded by an incredibly sweet—but surprisingly blank-eyed—smile.

Neal thought, wretchedly, that he had never had more of a duty to instill happiness in anyone—and less of a desire to do so. "We're approaching Four Corners," he said, "and the parsonage. The school, where we have church services, is that way half a mile. Just beyond is Royce's place, then mine. The whole country is laid out in sections, you see. Royce and I each have a quarter section . . . adjoining . . ."

His passenger gave him her attention, asking pertinent questions, her hands working the entire time, giving away her facade of control.

Neal pulled into the Victor yard, jumped down, tied the horse to the fence, and moved to the side of the buggy to help down the bride-to-be. Her hand trembled in his.

Looking at her gravely, Neal said, "Don't be afraid. Becky and I have prayed, and I'm sure the Lord heard and that everything will go according to His plan. Royce," he said to the pale face, "is waiting . . . just beyond that door."

Emmie Victor, the pastor's small daughter, opened the door, smiling a greeting and taking in the ravishing picture of the bride with girlish curiosity. "Go right on in," she whispered, "they're all ready."

At the sound of their approach Royce stepped forward,

his hands outstretched, his smile broad, his eyes alight.

Neal, watching at the bride's shoulder, saw his brother's smile become fixed, his eyes fill with dismay. Looking down into the white face bravely and proudly raised to him, Royce managed one word, spoken in a strangled tone.

"Meg!"

26

Luther Boggs pulled into the Lamb place, a cow tied behind the wagon and balancing beside him on the spring seat one of Lily's lemony suet puddings and three loaves of Miss P's potato bread.

Although it was early in the morning of the first day after the Lamb family's arrival, smoke was pouring from the stovepipe, and a boy and a girl were hanging on the rail fence beside the small log barn, a piece of grass in each mouth, their white legs bare and their soft feet wet with the morning's dew. Jumping down, they scampered toward the visitor.

"Good morning, little Lambs," Luther said, and the pair chuckled, looking up at him with happy, though pinched, faces.

"I'm Joe," the oldest child said, "and this is my sister Josie. Is that our cow?"

When Luther assured them it was and that he had been taking care of her until their arrival, the children danced to the rear of the rig and with eager but unpracticed hands tried to untie her.

"Her name is Faithful," Josie told Luther gravely. "Our dad wrote and told us about her. And she's going to have a calf."

"And we'll call it Prince if it's a boy or Princess if it's a girl," Joe finished for his sister.

"And I suppose you know the horses are Mister and Missus?" Luther asked. Apparently Jacob Lamb had a streak of playfulness in him. What a shame that he wasn't here to share it with his family!

"The horses are in the pasture," Luther advised them.

"Our brother, Jake, has been out to see them. He knows all about horses. He worked in the stables in Toronto. He even knows how to milk. And he's going to teach us."

"Well, he can start today. Faithful needs to be milked, and it will give you fresh milk right away." How eager Jacob Lamb had been to get his children on the farm and feed them properly. The garden was in and flourishing, chickens were laying, and the crop was up. Just how much Jake knew about raising a crop, Luther didn't know. But Miss P, who paid his wages, had outlined new responsibilities for him: help the Lamb family get things under control on their homestead.

Even as they spoke a tall thin teenaged boy approached.

"I'm Jake," he said briefly and shook hands like a man. "We thank you for taking care of our stock for us. I hope we'll be able to manage from now on. This," he said, motioning to a younger boy who had come from the house, "is Freddy. Between us we think we can make a go of it."

"I'll be here to help," Luther said, and together they made their way to the barn where Luther pointed out feed for chickens, grain for the horses, and outlined numerous activities that would get the boys started.

"If you can get settled and get a routine going where the chores are concerned, you'll find that things will fall into place. When it comes to Faithful having her calf and so on, I'll come if you'll send one of the kids. In fact, I'll come reg-

195

ularly and help you get organized here. Many a homesteader is not much older than you. About 18, aren't you?"

Jake, stretching it a little, said, "About."

"I hope the Missus is doing all right," Luther said with a
glance toward the house, and Jake assured him his mother
was doing as well as could be expected.

And then Luther said something that threw fear into all
of them and sent them running for the house as soon as Luther had delivered his bombshell and left: "Your neighbor,
Miss Partridge, is going to want to come over and meet
your Mum and see what she can do to help. You'll all love
Miss P."

"What'll we do? We can't let anyone know Mama isn't
here!" The questions tumbled from the frightened children.
"What if that Society lady comes or sends someone to look
into things here? Can she track us here? Can she? Can she?"

There was great panic in the small house; there were
tears on the part of the little ones, and Kerry clung to
Ammie's dress.

Plans were carefully laid. First, the family would go past
several homes, bunched together in the buggy, with Ammie
in her padding and Mama's hat plain for all to see. Then, at
home and dressed as herself, Ammie would greet visitors
and excuse Mama, saying she was ill or sick with grief and
unable to see company. It was the best they could think of.

And sure enough, a gaunt, stiff-backed but smiling lady
drove into the yard the next afternoon.

"I'm your neighbor, Miss Partridge," she said at the
door. "But everyone calls me Miss P. I've brought gingerbread—"

And when the door remained closed and she continued
talking through the screen, she said mildly, "May I come
in?"

Having met the children and taken a seat, Miss P seemed to find the conversation hard going. Finally she asked, "And how is Mrs. Lamb?"

Ammie cast a significant look toward the closed bedroom door. "Our mother is not well, Miss Partridge. I don't think she can visit with you today."

There seemed nothing left for Miss P to say or do, and eventually she took a somewhat awkward farewell.

The preacher fared no better. Back home, he told Ellie about it.

"The house is neat and nice . . . seems very homey," he said, "and the children appear to be thriving. But it's all done, I guess, without a mother's hand. She certainly wasn't in evidence when I was there. The girl Ammie explained that her mother is not well, has a problem with her chest, she said, but I didn't hear any sound of her. I invited them to Sunday School, but the boy—a young man, really—named Jake, said he thought they would wait until their mother was able to go with them."

The underfed bodies of the Lamb children filled out; they took on healthy tans, and, to a casual observer, things seemed to go on normally. Ammie, with Josie's help, kept the house tidy, saw that everyone had their scheduled bath, cut ragged hair, managed the washing—responsibilities she had borne in Toronto.

Meals were no problem. Papa had ground his own grain into flour, the cow gave an abundance of milk, and the garden—quickly the pride and joy of the city-bred children—produced the fresh green vegetables for which they had hungered.

With Luther's help, Jake learned to mow and rake, and winter's hay for the animals was assured. Looming always on the horizon was the threat of winter and the need for food for animal and family. And, as the grain ripened, there was an uneasiness concerning threshing day.

Miss P, being Miss P, couldn't leave well enough alone, of course. A sick mother . . . a houseful of children without close supervision . . . and no Sunday School!

And yet, time after time, when she called by, she was assured that Mama, though doing better, was still sick. Miss P left her goodies, tousled the heads of the little ones who gathered around her like bees to honey, and left—her concern, and then her suspicions, growing.

Finally there came a day when Miss P invited the children to her place. "Come meet Tom Bigbee," she urged. "He loves children. And Lily's cat—the best mouser in the world—has babies. I imagine Lily will let you have one when they are ready to leave their mother. What do you say to that?"

The children, being children, leaped and danced around Ammie and Jake and begged to go. After discussion, Jake and Ammie agreed that Joe and Josie could go. Freddy, only 11 and a boy at heart though he carried, in some ways, a man's load, looked so woebegone that Miss P issued a special invitation to him, and Jake and Ammie relented. "Remember," they privately warned all three just before they mounted Miss P's buggy, "nobody must know Mum isn't here with us!"

After a visit to the little house of Lily and Luther Boggs, where Lily's ankle had healed nicely, a tour of the barn and granary, an introduction to Old Mag and several calves, there was the promised visit to the corner stall where four small kittens mewed and wandered blindly amid the straw.

All of them, even Freddy, were moved to awe by the miracle of new birth. With Miss P's permission the babies were held and cuddled, named and renamed, and two of them were promised as theirs when the time came to leave their mother.

"She'll miss them dreffully," Josie said anxiously.

"We'll take good care of them, silly!" Freddy said quickly.

In Miss P's comfortable home, surrounded by Tom Bigbee, pillows, and popcorn, the children happily settled at Miss P's knee to be read to. First it was a chapter of *Black Beauty*, with a promise "to be continued," and then Miss P, ever so casually, picked up her Bible.

Miss P well remembered her ploy where the children's father, Jacob Lamb, had been concerned and her reverse application of doing unto others: She had inveigled Jacob into doing good unto her in order that she might—as was right and proper—do good unto him. Now, she figured, the same principle would work where Jacob's children and Sunday School were concerned: If they wouldn't go to Sunday School, Sunday School would come unto them!

Last Sunday's lesson had been about the three Hebrew children in the fiery furnace. Miss P explained the background, and then, in a passion unequalled by any fiery pulpiteer, delivered the herald's command: "To you it is commanded, O people, nations, and languages, that at what time ye hear the sound of the cornet, flute, harp, sackbut, psaltery, dulcimer, and all kinds of music, ye fall down and worship the golden image that Nebuchadnezzar the king hath set up: and whoso falleth not down and worshippeth shall the same hour be cast into the midst of a burning fiery furnace."

It was enough to widen the eyes of the fascinated children, and they waited with bated breath for the outcome.

199

With such an audience, could Miss P be less than her best? The rage of the king, the staunch faith of the three young men, the furnace "exceeding hot," and the king's astonished, "Lo, I see four men loose, walking in the midst of the fire, and they have no hurt; and the form of the fourth is like the Son of God," came alive to the small audience.

Finally, with "there is no other God that can deliver after this sort," great, deep breaths were expelled from three tense little bodies, and three cheers arose spontaneously.

After the clapping and the pleas for more, Miss P wisely turned to the 12th chapter of Luke and taught the three fatherless little waifs about their Heavenly Father's love. Now intimately familiar with sparrows, the application was timely and pertinent. The Heavenly Father knew when each tiny, unimportant bird fell, and He would care for them. "Fear not therefore: ye are of more value than many sparrows," they repeated after Miss P and went home with its comfort in their hearts.

Naturally such a pleasant time must be repeated. And how could Ammie and Jake resist the pleas of the little ones so long denied all such happy experiences?

After the story of Joseph cast into prison, Miss P taught the sympathetic children the passage from John 6:32—"I am not alone because the Father is with me," and she assured them that this promise was a great comfort to anyone who felt lonely or forsaken by the loss of their earthly father. "Like me," she said.

As the days came and went, it seemed to be an understood thing that Miss P could sit in the Lamb house and visit and talk, read to the children, take tea, and never seem to be unduly concerned that a sick woman was bedbound just the other side of the wall. The children's tension eased considerably, and they no longer feared she would question them further or perhaps insist on visiting the ailing woman.

Occasionally Jake felt it necessary for Ammie to don the disguise and he would drive around Wildrose, his "mother" at his side. Once as Miss P crossed her yard, the fictitious Mrs. Lamb even waved in response to Miss P's greeting.

"Now she'll be sure and ask to see Mum!" Jake groaned, and Ammie looked frightened at the very thought. But the next time Miss P came, she merely asked that they be sure and assure their mother that she would do all she could to help see that the children were well and happy, and that was that.

Josie's one good dress needed mending, and Miss P patched it. Little Kerry, with all that good food and milk, grew rapidly, and Miss P produced two new dresses for her. Miss P accompanied the children on berry picking outings and spent hot, steamy hours helping Ammie make jelly and sauce. Luther, at Miss P's suggestion, showed Jake how to kill a chicken and Ammie how to clean it and prepare it for roasting. And all without any snooping and prying into the bedfast Mrs. Lamb and her mysterious ailment.

Ammie wrote her mother faithfully and letters arrived from Toronto from time to time. Ammie's letters were full of Miss P, whom the children soon began calling Aunt Phoebe, and there came a day when, after Miss P had made a pan of candy, shared a cup of tea, and sung little Kerry to sleep, that Ammie was able to say, with complete honesty, "Mama says to thank you for all you do for us."

27

While the wedding party gaped, Royce Ferguson stared down at—not an expected imperious, bewitching, intoxicating face—but one that was, rather than fascinating, demure and winsome. It was a comely face but not exquisite; bonny but not breathtaking. The eyes, hazel rather than blue, looked back at him with a mixture of sensitivity and bravado, but there was no teasing or tantalizing. And Royce was expecting breathtaking, teasing, and tantalizing.

Meg hadn't known what to expect. Disappointment, of course, perhaps chagrin or hurt; she was even prepared for anguish over Marlys's inconstancy. But with Royce's gasped "Meg!" she was totally unprepared for the accompanying ugly red stain that flooded the handsome, eager face.

Meg so keenly felt Royce's staggering surprise that she put a quick, sympathetic hand on his arm. With a hoarse cry he shook it off, put a hand to his brow, and managed, "Is this some kind of a joke? Where is Marlys?" And he looked wildly beyond Meg and around the room.

"Meg?" Neal was repeating uncomprehendingly.

"Meg!" Becky was exclaiming. "Meg! Meg!"

Gerald Victor laid aside the church manual he had been holding and stepped forward.

"Royce," he said quietly, and his voice had the effect of

bringing the shaken man to some semblance of normalcy. "I gather there is some sort of problem here?"

"Problem? Problem? It's just that Marlys hasn't come! It's just that she's sent a substitute! Can you imagine that?" Royce's voice took on a half-hysterical note. "A substitute bride!"

"It isn't quite like that—" Meg began.

"Everyone—my mother, Becky—told me she would never marry me! I dared to believe she meant what she said! I staked my future on it! Surely this is just a delay. Is it," he asked with sudden hope, "one of those proxy arrangements? Tell me she'll be here yet!"

Meg looked sick but steady. "She's not coming, Royce. Not now, not ever."

"What happened . . . what did she say? Her letter . . . it sounded so sure, so positive. How could she change so quickly?"

When Meg remained silent, he said slowly, "You wrote for her, didn't you?"

"But not behind her back. She asked me to."

How to tell the stunned man that Marlys had been much more interested in present company than in an absent admirer. How could she put into words the supreme casualness Marlys had shown when, at the last, Meg had said, "Well, then, I'm going to go in your place!"

With a careless laugh Marlys had said, "I bequeath the farmer to you, my dear sister. Have him, with my blessings. You've never seemed to mind being second-best."

Marlys's ticket, Marlys's trunk, Marlys's wedding gifts from family and skeptical friends—all were grandly bequeathed. Marlys's husband . . .

For Royce was saying, bitterly, with supreme casualness, "Why not? Let the games begin! Step into place, Becky,

203

Neal! Say the words, Reverend, that will tie some kind of magical, mystical knot that makes a man and woman one. My dear," he said with elaborate formality, bowing to Meg, "will you do me the honor of becoming my wife?"

Startled, dismayed, Meg was silent before his cynicism.

"I think not, Royce," Pastor Victor was saying. "I'm not prepared to unite in marriage a man in your present mood. It is to be entered into advisedly . . ."

"Rejected twice in the same day!" Royce said in an amused tone. "That's got to be some kind of record."

Neal moved at last, stepping forward and putting his hand on his brother's shoulder. Becky's move was toward Meg. Sympathy, hilarity, and excitement battled for expression on her round face. But it was with admiration she put her arms around her friend and whispered, "Welcome to Wildrose, Meg! But what a way to get here!"

The best arrangement seemed to be for Meg to go home with Becky. "Meg and I can bunk together," Becky said practically, "and Neal and Royce. After all, we have two houses."

At the buggies there was considerable awkwardness. Finally Becky rode with Royce and Meg with Neal.

Following a grim-faced Royce from the parsonage yard, Meg offered, in a thoughtful voice, "I should have had your advice—about praying I mean—before I came all this way. But it was either me or . . . no bride at all. I thought," Meg continued in a small voice, "a second-best bride might be better than no bride at all. I certainly misjudged the depth of Royce's feelings for Marlys. Somehow I was led to believe he felt no more deeply about the union than she did."

"What," Neal asked, "will you do now?"

"Do? Why follow through. There's no rush, is there? I'm just happy to be here!" and Meg breathed deeply and looked around with satisfaction. "Many a woman has come out to marry a man she hasn't met . . . it happens all the time. I don't see why it won't work out well yet, for Royce and me. He wants . . . needs a wife; I'm here. And this time, I'll do as you suggested—pray."

"And I," Neal said thoughtfully, "will pray too."

28

The two Ferguson homesteads were almost mirror images of each other. With the section line directly between, but unmarked, just a few hundred feet separated the cabins, and, back of them, the barns, granaries, corrals, and chicken coops. Almost halfway between, perhaps on the line, one well served both places. On one side, Neal's trough; on the other, Royce's.

To Meg, standing on the small covered stoop of Royce's house, surveying the tranquil scene, it seemed the ultimate in satisfaction; who could want more? On every hand were evidences of hard, even grueling, work; Royce and Neal Ferguson had literally grub-hoed their clearings into existence. Their hands, and those of neighbors committed to helping one another, had erected the buildings. The two brothers had not only finished them, first one and then another—back and forth—but had dug their well, planted their gardens, raised their small but developing herds and flocks. Having done none of it, still Meg reveled in the sense of gratification that had to be the natural reaction of any pioneer heart.

To the north stretched the Canadian Shield, attracting little or no interest as farmland. With its small soil cover and cold climate, it was not conducive to lush growth. Lichen, scrub oak, and spruce forest covered the area, with heavier, boreal forest as one moved south.

To the south of Wildrose lay the vast stretches of prairie—the grasslands, crisscrossed with the soon-to-be-forgotten tracks of Red River carts and prairie schooners and dotted sparsely with soddies.

And in between—and delightful to Meg—an area where the Plains meet the Shield, called the Parkland. Its virgin bush stretched thickly, a challenge indeed to a settler; its soil was black and rich, but its frost-free season was scarcely more than 100 days. Late June or early August frosts were not unknown.

The Saskatchewan River, the great highway of the fur trade, lay between the rich fur lands of the northern forest and the plains, until recently so thronged with buffalo. Its tawny water flowed just a few miles from the Ferguson farms. And about 20 miles away—the developing and growing settlement named for the Queen's consort—Prince Albert. The coming of the railroad had made it possible to freight in settlers' goods that previously had to be carted or rafted. Cattle, farm implements, household effects, all packed into one car while the family traveled in the "colonist car," bringing their bedding with them, sleeping on wooden bunks, cooking their own meals.

Life, for the frontier people, was hard. They all suffered a sense of isolation. There was little money, and heads of households often had to augment their income by working away from home in a lumber camp or on the railroad, increasing the wife's anxieties and doubling her workload.

While there was no real shortage of food, the diet often palled, lacking variety. Wild game abounded; spring was welcomed for its dandelion greens and lamb's-quarters and its promise of berries for jams and jellies.

Doctors were few and far between; the Mounted Police had a medical officer who often served as doctor for the settler. Most injuries and ailments were cared for by father, mother, a neighbor, or local midwife, whose expertise was called on for cuts and gashes, crushed bones and fractured skulls, and whose drugstore was the catalog.

With all its hardships, the promise of free land sent a powerful message worldwide. It was land, the Cree said, that was created by a muskrat from a bit of earth, the rat having been sent out from a raft the legendary Wee-sack-ka-chack had built to save the animals from a great flood. It was land coveted by men who had none and treasured by those who claimed a piece of it for themselves.

To Meg, it seemed a million miles and a thousand years away from the city, where lamplighters trudged streets, leaving gaslight flickering for the dark night; where the streets were thronged with people, walking, riding in carts, carriages, and even electric cars; where gentlemen strolled in Prince Albert suits, fancy silk vests, and hats—fedora, derby, crusher, nutria fur. Where women paraded in high fashion capes, tailor-made walking suits, cashmere shawls of weblike consistency, their heads piled with hair and hat, covered from rain or sun with an umbrella or parasol, and mincing along on narrow, pointed, kid shoes.

Meg eyed the lantern hanging handily by the door, the galvanized tub beside it, and the path leading off to the outhouse and remembered the well-to-do city houses with their telephones, indoor toilets, electric lights, and central heating.

And often, parked beside the house—a bicycle! Meg watched a boy on a horse, riding bareback down the road, and waved as was the custom, and the happy hordes of bicycle riders seemed to people another world, another time.

Breathing air fragrant with a mix of wildflowers, leaf mold, wood shavings, and clover, Meg knew she would not trade it for anything else the wide world might have to offer. That she was actually here was incredible. That she stay, imperative!

And Royce, once the shock of Marlys's rejection had worn off, was, at first, philosophical then deigning to accept the fact that Meg was alive, was pleasant, and was *here*.

About the third day, Meg and Royce talked about Marlys. Though it seemed to hurt, he wanted to know how and why Marlys had changed her mind.

Gently, Meg introduced the fact that Marlys probably never had any intention of coming and was happily . . . diverted now.

"Just playing," Royce brooded, and Meg didn't try to defend what she knew to be true.

"It's her nature, Royce," she had said honestly. "To her it is a game, and she doesn't really understand men who don't know how to play it."

They were sitting side by side on the steps, and Royce cast his gaze around the crude homestead, trying to see it through other eyes. "She wouldn't have liked it," he said finally. "And I would have known it . . . and that would have hurt as much, maybe more . . ." His voice trailed away.

And though Meg waited patiently, he said no more but walked away to expend his strength, and his misery, in chopping wood for the insatiable range.

There came a time, at the supper table, when Becky and Meg were laughing and joking, and Royce's eyes, for just a moment, crinkled with humor. Meg saw it and was content. Neal, across the table, saw it too and nodded significantly at Meg. Royce, Neal thought, was healing, but whether from disappointment or chagrin, he wasn't sure. Never having met Marlys, Neal couldn't judge, but to his way of thinking, Royce had a prime choice sitting at the same table. His brother's happiness was of first importance to Neal. Though he had grieved with him and wondered what sort of a girl would offer herself, unasked and apparently unwanted, to a man, he soon found his early opinion of Meg—made in the buggy on the ride from Meridian—reasserting itself. Here, he felt, was a woman with all the qualities of a homesteader. And good-natured as well! A girl who would brighten long lonely winter evenings, cheer a man's heart when things were discouraging, and make a simple home a place of warmth and charm.

"Are you praying?" Meg asked Neal privately, reminding him of their earlier conversation.

"Every day," he assured her. "And you?"

"I'm . . . I'm learning to," Meg said a little shyly. "I do see its importance. The hardest part—"

"The hardest part?"

"The hardest part is 'Thy will be done.' What if . . . what if His will isn't what I want?"

"I like the comfort of the verse that says, 'None of them that trust in him shall be desolate.' That must mean His plan will be a good one, without a need to be downcast or woebegone—"

"Or disappointed?"

"Or disappointed. The apostle Paul said the kingdom of God is 'righteousness, and peace, and joy in the Holy Ghost.' "

"All the things I want."

"We all do. And I guess the person who has these is one satisfied being. Does anything else really matter?"

Meg turned from that conversation thoughtfully, finding, in the backwoods, reason for a joy she hadn't known existed and a contentment not dependent on place or person.

Meg and Becky romped through the days, finding pleasure in everything. Nighttime found them worn but happy. Morning found them filled with zest. Royce's spirits picked up, his laugh once again joining the others'.

There came a Sunday when, ready to mount the two buggies and go to church, Royce casually helped Meg into his rig for the first time.

Becky and Neal, in Neal's buggy, saw the significance in this move on their brother's part, and each heaved a sigh. One was a sigh of relief and satisfaction.

29

Ammie and Jake were using the morning for a buggy ride to Meridian. Here Ammie would sell a few eggs and purchase some supplies; but the main reason for going was to mail a letter to Mum and to see whether or not she had written to them.

Reports from Amanda had been encouraging; perhaps it was the contented reports from her children, allowing her, for the first time in months, to relax, rest, eat, and grow strong. But Amanda knew they couldn't carry on long without an adult; Jake might be doing a man's work, but Ammie was too young, too young! She couldn't continue carrying the workload. Amanda thought of a certain Miss P with mixed feelings—an uneasiness, combined with passionate gratefulness. The uneasiness was natural, for what, after all, did she really know of this strange woman? (At times, in response to the children's uninhibited reports of this woman's antics and performances, she did indeed come across as strange.) Far away and helpless, Amanda could only hope Miss P's influence was a good one; certainly she gave evidence of a good heart. The children's ploy to keep everyone unaware that their mother was not with them made Amanda uneasy too. But all this she tried to put aside when she wrote, giving instead, encouragement and hope that one day soon she would be with them.

The buggy held two comfortably. It was, therefore, a relief to Jake and Ammie when Miss P suggested a day of "nature study." The smaller children were enthralled. Loving their new home as they did, having surrendered to its beauty and bounty rapidly, and knowing little or nothing of its hardships, they were eager to become better acquainted with it. And who better to tell them than Miss P?

They waved good-bye to Ammie and Jake and never thought to begrudge them the visit to the hamlet; they had had enough of "towns," though Meridian fell far short of that distinction.

Miss P wore a straw hat with a wide, flopping brim and carried her father's cane for purposes of pointing, digging, moving things. At times it served as an extension of her long bony finger; at times, like a machete, it slashed and thrust a way through thick growth.

Freddy carried the picnic basket manfully, his red hair reflecting the morning sun with shafts of light; freckles, new freckles, emerged almost by the minute. His feet, like his younger siblings', were bare. His knee pants revealed scratched brown legs. The sleeves of his navy blue duck blouse with its wide sailor collar had been hacked off raggedly to reveal scratched, brown arms.

Joe and Josie, equally brown and equally scratched and happily so, clutched the hands of Kerry. Now four years old, this was the first outing Kerry had been permitted; Ammie had not been willing to trust Kerry's naïveté regarding their mother's supposed presence in the bedroom. But through numerous appallingly frank comments from the child ("Mama will like this when she comes," "I'm saving all of these egg shells for Mama," "My mama said this . . . my mama said that"), Miss P had remained amazingly hard of hearing and stoical.

Now skipping along between her brother and sister, Kerry piped, and more than once, "Let's show this to Mama when she comes." Joe and Josie had held their breath and looked quickly at Miss P; Freddy had frowned at them and put his finger to his lips. And sure enough, Miss P exhibited her recurring tendency to deafness and marched blithely on.

The children had all been particularly entranced with the "darling" chipmunk. So tiny, so quick, so bright-eyed, so daring, it was an impudent invader of yard and garden and even now flickered around them, scampering along the ground or overhead on tree branches.

"I just love chipmugs," Kerry piped.

Miss P stopped the cavalcade and pointed the cane at a particularly brave and curious "chipmug," its beady eyes fixed on the lifted faces below its leafy perch. Its handlike claws were clasped to its chest in the charming fashion so beguiling to everyone with an eye to stop and watch. Its little face was striped light and dark, and black stripes edged with white curved down its tiny body; its underparts were pale.

The narrow face was stuffed to the point of bulging with its foraging—seeds, berries, nuts in season, sometimes insects.

"Little pig!" murmured Josie fondly.

"It has to push all that food out of its cheeks with its forepaws," Miss P explained in a quiet voice, and the chipmunk frisked its tail.

"Let's see if we can find its burrow," Miss P said and poked with her stick, moving growth until a mound of dirt caught their attention. There, in a clump of bushes, was the small opening to the burrow.

Miss P pointed out its tiny size—about two inches in diameter.

"It hides its burrow like this," she said, "so foxes and dogs and coyotes and hawks won't find it. It probably lives alone down there for its lifetime—three years, if it's lucky. It will go down there in November and stay there probably until March."

"Is he going to put that pouchful of food down there?" asked Joe.

"He's busy, saving for winter—"

"Just like us," Josie said wisely, thinking of the vegetables and berries they were beginning to store away in the cellar under their kitchen.

"Perhaps three feet down," Miss P explained, "it has its main chamber, and it could be big enough to hold as much as half a bushel of food."

"That's a lot of work," Joe said, having just helped trundle carrots to their cellar and still aching from the task.

"Yes, and we better get along and let him empty that load." And the group moved on through the grasses and bush. Overhead the poplars quivered, casting shifting shadows on the earnest, happy faces of the new Wildrosers.

The children paused at a growth of birches, peeling its bark off in thin, papery sheets, stuffing some in pockets, "to see if we can write on them."

"Ah," Miss P said, "we're in luck." And she pointed out the small red fruit of the bearberry. "Kinni-kinnick is the Indian word. They boiled the plant for tea." Still being in bloom, the idea of tea was regretfully forsaken.

Black-eyed Susans grew abundantly and therefore received no more than a glance. Bluebells, though plentiful, came in for much oohing and ahing because of their daintiness. "They grow almost anyplace," Miss P said fondly, "and may even bloom as late as September. They're tough, I guess, like the people who choose to live here."

"We choose to live here!" the children chorused.

Even the common dandelion came under close scrutiny.

"A nuisance!" Freddy, the incipient farmer, stated flatly.

"A pest!" Joe, the reluctant gardener, agreed.

"Valuable!" Miss P declared and got their attention. "Its leaves have been used in salads for years and years. And if you needed a laxative, I could make you one from the roots."

The children affirmed their present state of good health.

"It's great food for moose, grouse, partridge, and even bear," Miss P continued. "And see—" she pointed out the indentations on the leaves, "its leaves are shaped like lions' teeth. That's why it takes its name from the French expression *dents de lion*."

The children were impressed by the lion connection.

"Now we'll gather some of these," Miss P said, pointing out, with her cane, the spreading milkweed. "You'll just have to eat something from our tour today, and it might as well be this. Pick off the flowers," she instructed, "and when we get home I'll fry them in batter. The young leaves and flower buds are delicious boiled, but we'll forget them today; they have to have several changes of water and we may not have time. It may be early for seed pods, but if you find any, nip them off, they are very tasty baked."

Intrigued, the children nipped and picked until Miss P declared they had "enough to feed threshers," which seemed to indicate a very great amount indeed. They had seen Jake testing the wheat for maturing, and they had seen and understood Ammie's uneasiness when the matter of feeding the threshers was mentioned. Sometimes Ammie was so tired that she was no fun at all! Once, when Josie had reproached her with it, Ammie had burst into tears, shocking them all. Jake had tried awkwardly to comfort her.

"Things are just getting ahead of me," Ammie had sniffled. "I never took care of a garden before or tried to put things away for winter. I see all those sealers down there in the cellar, and I don't know how to get the food from the garden and the bush into them!" And Ammie's tears had flowed afresh.

"I know," Jake had said. "The job's too big for me too. If it wasn't for Luther, I don't know what I'd do. We'll just learn as we go, I guess."

But Ammie's little frame was too fragile for the workload thrust on it now. And the more she heard of the winter, the more she feared it and fretted. Winter clothes! Enough food! Fuel for the range and heater!

The ride in the buggy to Meridian was blissful to Ammie. Not only did she have an opportunity to absorb the beauty and peacefulness of the bush but just lean back, let her hands be idle in her lap, and, perhaps, if the jolting wasn't too much, nod off to sleep. Another part of her had watched the children run off with Miss P, lighthearted and free, and had envied them. God bless Miss P! What would they do without her. With her, Ammie dared hope they might make it until Mum came.

At noontime Miss P and the children spread out their lunch at the side of a slough. Miss P took the opportunity to explain the difference between a loon and a duck.

"I know," Josie said, "a loon cries and a duck quacks." They had all been startled upon first hearing the long, lonely cry of the loon.

"Only one pair of loons settle on any one lake," Miss P explained. "And it has to be a lake, not a slough, because they need up to a quarter of a mile to get into the air. They almost seem to run across the water, neck stretched and wings aflap, trying to get into the air. A duck's wings are large in relation to its body, and it can launch itself quickly, lifting almost straight up."

They watched the ducks in the lake, many of them babies, recently hatched. To get a closer view and perhaps find a nest or two in the rushes, Joe, Josie, and Kerry, having finished the last boiled egg and taken a last sip of milk from the communal jar, went to the water's edge to play, watch, and discover.

Miss P, sitting on the grassy ground, was throwing crumbs to the frisky chipmunks and a wily jay that had announced its presence with boisterous calls.

"Aunt Phoebe—," Freddy began, toying with the milk jar.

"Yes, Freddy?" Miss P gave the boy her full attention, alerted perhaps by the extreme casualness of his tone.

"Those Ten Commandments you've been teaching us—"

"The 'thou shalts' and the 'thou shalt nots.' "

"Were they just for the people who lived in Old Testament times?"

"I believe Jesus spoke about most of them, and that's in the New Testament."

"So they'd be for us today?"

"I'd say so, yes."

"That one—about stealing. 'Thou shalt not steal,' it says. In the Old Testament."

"When Jesus was talking to a young man—the rich young ruler, he's called—He said, 'Thou knowest the commandments,' and He mentioned several, among them 'Do not steal.' "

Freddy was agitating the bottle and its small remaining supply of milk until, had it been cream, he might have ended up with butter. Miss P watched silently.

"But if a person was . . . was hungry, would stealing be wrong?"

"I think the Lord who said He'd supply all our needs would find a different way to meet that need. If a person asked Him."

"And God forgives sins like that?"

"Washes them away. Makes a person—inside—whiter than snow. Than milk even."

Freddy buried his freckled face between his two knees. "I need that to happen to me," he said fiercely. "I need it bad!"

"Why, Freddy, you're no worse than me or anyone else. The Bible says all have sinned and come short of the glory of God."

"Even you, Aunt Phoebe?" Freddy dared raise his face to look at his angelic Miss P with wondering eyes.

"*Especially* me. I felt like my heart was very black indeed. What a relief it was to be forgiven!"

"I guess so!" Freddy said fervently.

"And you know the really great news, Freddy? God says He will remember those sins against us no more. They are buried in the sea of His forgetfulness, never to be brought up again."

With a choked sob, Freddy said, "I need that, Aunt Phoebe—so *bad!*"

And the boy, burdened with the wrong he had done and unable to forget it, crept through the grasses to Miss P's outstretched hand. Never had a bony knee seemed more like an altar; never had the skies been more open; never had the fragrance of the bush more beautifully typified the sweetness of a soul forgiven. Never had a young heart been more in earnest; never had God been more faithful.

The bottom hem of Miss P's voluminous skirt wiped away the repentant tears. Miss P's tender hand stroked the glowing head still pressed against her knee. Miss P's whisper, half-choked with tears, was lifted to heaven: "Thank You, Father, that this little Lamb has come into the fold."

Then, head cocked, ears—inner ears—hearing very clearly, it seemed, Miss P nodded. "Ah, yes, Lord—those other sheep You have. Them also."

30

The all-too-brief summer slipped away all too quickly. Meg spent it in a whirl of busyness. She and Becky, both greenhorns in some ways, had much to learn. They had, of course, experience with gardens and with canning but not to the extent needed for a winter season in an isolated homestead. Caring for milk was new to both of them, with its churning and making of cheese. Neither had ever cared for chickens or turkeys or ducks; never had they set broody hens.

Picking the bush's berries—saskatoon, gooseberry, pin cherry, chokecherry, cranberry, and strawberry (raspberries were invariably wormy)—offered some lighter moments. The girls experienced every pioneer woman's satisfaction in cellar shelves filling with freely provided bounty.

Meg loved the bush; the hours spent in it were sheer pleasure. She felt so at home in it that she might have considered herself an oldtimer, if she hadn't been so abysmally ignorant about this immense land she now called home.

She knew Canada was a wide and awesome land stretching between two islands, one on the east, the other on the west. To the north, glaciers and tundra; to the south, a vigorous neighbor. That it was a land of towering peaks, flowing waters, and sun-splashed meadows, she knew. That it was a place of vast wilderness, deep forests, and endless prairies, she knew.

Dimly she recognized that it was a land of men and women of indomitable courage, who intimately knew hardship and despair as they faced raging prairie fires, persistent winds, subzero temperatures and harsh blizzards, hordes of mosquitoes, hailstones, and crop failure on a regular basis. But she knew, too, that when the crocus bloomed again and the meadowlark sang its siren song, courage and hope revived; the plow thrust its blade once more in the beckoning land with its tantalizing promise of fecundity, and they went doggedly on.

But for Meg, this land was the pungent smells of trees, flowers, ripening grain, berries shriveling in the sun, and hay drying in the meadows. It was the bawl of a cow and the rough tongue of a calf twined around an extended finger. It was the nighttime howl of a lonely coyote, the sweep of a hundred and more redwing blackbirds as they settled on the rustling reeds of a slough. It was the loon's eerie yodel echoing across a lake in the evening and a meadowlark trilling from the sky at morning's first light. It was early rising, full days, and sweet slumber.

It was Royce, looking at her more and more with interest and favor. It was Neal . . .

It was Neal obviously making occasions for her to be with Royce, for a carefree walk around the homestead, a buggy ride to Meridian, a time alone after supper while he and Becky, at his suggestion, made themselves scarce.

It would have taken a blind man not to see that Meg was a true pioneer spirit. She worked willingly and cheerfully; she took the long look, being a dreamer of dreams, and keeping the goal in mind rather than the moment's discouragement. She wore well. The trio of siblings never felt uncomfortable with her presence.

Once, hesitatingly but rather anxiously, Becky had asked, "Do you ever think of . . . going back, Meg?"

"Never!" Meg spoke with the voice of one who has looked at the alternative and made her choice. "But, Becky . . . I can't just stay on here indefinitely. Here with you and Royce and Neal, that is."

Meg bit her lip, worrying the idea around and around in her mind as she had on numerous occasions since Royce's refusal of her as his bride. Somehow she hadn't been prepared for that; she had truly thought Royce's attachment for Marlys was superficial. She sighed now and Becky, perhaps understanding, pursued the subject she had introduced.

"Royce is . . . is coming 'round, I think."

Meg was silent. The idea of Royce "coming 'round" was, somehow, belittling.

But it was what she had come for. Squaring her shoulders and summoning a smile, Meg said, "I'll give it a little longer, Becky. Now—perhaps if I made him a chocolate cake for supper?" Becky giggled, as Meg had hoped she would, and the subject was dropped. At least between the girls.

To Royce, however, Becky said, having walked to the barn where he was preparing to milk that evening, "I think Meg is beginning to feel a little uncomfortable staying here with us for so long a time. And it's all your fault!" Becky looked at her brother accusingly. "You have a responsibility here, Royce!"

Startled, Royce looked at his sister.

"Well, it isn't as if Marlys were ever going to come!"

"Hmmm . . ." Royce went back to his milking.

That evening Becky thought Royce looked at Meg seriously, thoughtfully.

"Would you take a walk to the meadow with me when the chores are all done, Meg?"

Although it was not an unusual request, there was a tenseness about Royce . . . his voice perhaps . . . that caused Meg's heart to skip a beat.

With Royce gone from the table and Becky fixing dishwater, Meg paused at Neal's side and said, rather breathlessly, "I've been praying . . . like you said, but now . . . now that it looks like it might happen . . . I wonder . . ." And Meg looked for her answer in the face of the young man.

But when he said, "It's what you've wanted . . . remember that. Royce has been worth waiting for," and she saw the honest, earnest look in his gray eyes, she firmed her surprisingly weak knees, drew a deep breath, and strengthened her resolve. After all, she had prayed. And Neal had prayed; all would go as the Lord intended.

And so it was with a measure of peace Meg walked out into the long evening with Royce, crossing the yard, entering the bush, and making for the fragrant meadow with its recumbent cattle and frolicking calves.

"Sit down, Meg," Royce said finally, pointing out a fallen log.

Sitting beside her, his hands hanging between his knees, his eyes fixed on the horizon, Royce said the words Meg had been waiting to hear.

"Meg, will you do me the honor of marrying me?"

31

Freddy, being Freddy, could not keep silent about his new-found peace.

"See," he said earnestly to Ammie and Jake one night after the three younger children were in bed, "I have this good, clean feeling inside. Where before, I felt sort of dirty—you know, about taking that milk and not paying for it." Freddy's eyes still held a haunted look when he talked about it, and his brother and sister realized for the first time the full extent of the guilt he had borne.

"And this happened because of a prayer?" Ammie asked, half incredulous.

"Not a prayer like Mum used to say at mealtimes," Freddy explained, "nor like 'Now I lay me.' Oh!" he said, frustrated, "I don't know how to explain it! But it happened, anyway!"

And Ammie and Jake, knowing Freddy, believed him. This prayer—could they pray it too?

On Miss P's next visit, she laid a cloth-wrapped bundle on the table. Under the curious eyes of the Lamb children she opened it, revealing a Bible.

"It was mine when I was a little girl," she explained, and they all reached out and touched it reverently.

Though Jake had to go to work, the others gathered

around to hear the words of this new, old Book. Chosen thoughtfully by Miss P, who loved it well, the words were precious indeed.

And the pictures! Miss P found that they loved, above all, the picture of Jesus and the children.

"Look how they lean on Him!"

"See how He holds them . . . touches them!"

And they sat entranced at the "really-truly" story of this Man who had loved little children. "Suffer the little children to come unto me," Miss P read, "and forbid them not."

"Suffer?" Joe was puzzled.

"It means 'let them come, and don't hinder them,' " Miss P explained and added the words that made their eyes grow starry: "And he took them up in his arms, put his hands on them, and blessed them."

Understanding their need for love and their emptiness over the loss of their father, Miss P, on her next visit, read them the story of the prodigal son.

Freddy, who usually managed to avoid his work when Miss P came in order to sit in on the sessions, said triumphantly, "See! That's the way it was, with me!" And his sisters and brothers began to glimpse, though dimly, the monumental change that had happened to their Freddy.

Between visits, which seemed to be happening daily now, Miss P left the precious Book, and they were allowed to read it for themselves.

"Look here," Freddy said one evening, wanting to explain his personal miracle to the others, "God says if you don't touch the unclean thing . . . like stealing milk, I guess that means . . . He will receive you and be a Father unto you. 'Ye shall be my sons and daughters,' He says."

"I need a father," Josie piped hopefully. The faces of the

others reflected the same need and the same hope.

With the expectant faces fixed on him, what was a boy to do? Manfully and honestly, Freddy instructed them to bow their heads. Then the little missionary led them in a prayer of confession—

"But, Freddy!" Josie protested, "I didn't steal any milk!"

"You don't always mind Mum, do you?" Freddy asked reasonably. "And didn't you pinch Joe the other day when you got mad at him, and—"

Face guilty, Josie bowed.

As the little group prayed, the One who is the "father of the fatherless" kept His promise and assured them, not in words heard by the human ear but by the hungry heart, "Ye shall be my sons and daughters." To anyone with a tender, believing heart, it was not hard to picture the loving Jesus there in their midst, once again putting His hands on children and blessing them.

When Miss P came next, it was to be met by happy-faced, excited Lambs. Each in his or her own way tried to tell what had happened.

"We prayed, Aunt Phoebe, *really*, I mean."

"We all said we were sorry—"

"Now we have a Father, haven't we, Aunt Phoebe?"

There wasn't much work done on the Lamb homestead that day. The children had so many questions to ask, so many accounts to tell.

When a reluctant Miss P said good-bye, she hugged them all. "Keep reading the Book," she urged, and they chorused their decision to do so. "And remember," she told them, "you are never alone. Jesus said, 'Lo, I am with you always.' "

Running along at Miss P's side, Josie piped, "What's 'lo' mean, Aunt Phoebe?"

Climbing into the buggy and picking up the reins and filled to overflowing with the wonder of it all, Miss P's response welled up spontaneously.

"It means," she said, "fancy that!"

Through the days and weeks and months of summer and into the busy days of fall, Miss P, the perennial advocate of God's Word, mixed wise portions of it throughout the hours of work she spent on the Lamb place. Luther and Lily, shaking their heads but knowing their Miss P well, willingly did the work on the Partridge place. Miss P often had reason to bless Uncle Roscoe and the funds he had provided, not only for her own needs and the pay of Luther and now Lily but also for additional needs that sprang up on the Lamb homestead, which Miss P met in such a casual way the children little suspected her help and their dependence on it.

And never once did Miss P pry into the secret of the closed bedroom door, and the older children kept up an occasional lame reference to it and to their sick mother.

But in the way the Lord has, this feeble fabrication was exposed to be dealt with.

In his perusal of the Bible, Freddy was particularly taken with the parable of the sower. Having so recently experienced the amazing results of planting and harvesting, he reveled in the story of the planted seed and how some fell on good ground, some on bad, some among thorns, some springing up only briefly.

Reading it for the fifth or sixth time, Freddy was startled by one word: *honest*. A good and honest heart, the Bible said, was the ground that brought forth fruit.

Honest. Freddy knew he mustn't steal; now he wondered about other forms of dishonesty. Like lying.

After supper, Freddy gathered the family around his knees (in approved Miss P style) and opened the Bible to the eighth chapter of Luke, reading the parable aloud. Finishing it, he looked up, searching the innocent faces of his siblings.

"An honest and a good heart," he repeated with emphasis.

The children nodded complacently.

"Don't you get it?" Freddy asked impatiently.

"We have good hearts . . . now," Joe said patiently.

"Yes, but do we have *honest* hearts?" And Freddy turned and looked, meaningfully, at the bedroom door, closed, as always, on a mother who wasn't there.

The eyes of the other five turned, as one pair, to the door. As one pair they turned back, stricken with the truth of what Freddy had said.

"Sit down, Aunt Phoebe," Jake said the next morning when Miss P had laid aside her hat and the basket of clean clothes she had brought from home, fresh from Lily's scrub board and iron.

Miss P, usually filled with laughter and good cheer, looked at the sober faces gathered around her and settled back with a prayer of thanks; they were ready to make a clean breast of it and, in so doing, lift a heavy load from not only their shoulders but also their hearts.

"You see, Aunt Phoebe," Jake said as spokesman, pacing back and forth before the group, six pairs of eyes following him, five anxiously, one pair with gentle understanding, "we haven't been honest—"

"It's about our mum!" Josie broke in.

"She's not here . . . hasn't been here . . . the bedroom is empty . . . we haven't meant to be bad, Aunt Phoebe"—all

229

this and more poured forth from the confessing children.

And nothing would do but that they take Miss P to the door and let her see for herself.

"The boys sleep here at night," they explained, "but it's empty all day."

Reseating herself, Miss P invited, "Suppose you tell me all about it."

As the story unfolded and Miss P realized the depth of the fear the children had carried concerning being separated, and their anxiety over the "Society lady" that might find them even here, and she recalled their bravery in carrying on in the face of their aloneness, she breathed a silent prayer of thanks to their Heavenly Father and felt humbly grateful that she had so diligently pursued an acquaintance with their earthly father, opening a door for attention to his family when they came.

"I do believe that woman *lives* over there," Lily grumbled but not unkindly. She and Luther had also half adopted the "poor little lambs," and their presence had kept the summer filled with interest.

"I don't know how she'll stand it whenever their mother comes," Luther said with a shake of his head. "She'll be happy for them and, of course, it's the best thing that could happen, but my oh my—she'll be at loose ends for sure."

For sure enough, there came a day when Miss P was met by a dancing, screeching, excited group of children.

"Our mum's coming!"

"She's well . . . she's on her way!"

"Oh, Aunt Phoebe . . . Oh! Oh! Oh!"

Over the heads of the smaller children Miss P saw the tears of a tired but still gallant Ammie. And behind her, blinking hard, the desperately relieved face of the boy-man who had carried a load and a responsibility far too heavy for his age.

"I'm so glad . . . for you," Miss P murmured over and over again, hearing the story of their flight again, reading Amanda Lamb's letter, and helping to make plans for her welcome.

Riding home—alone and somehow more lonely than she had remembered—Miss P bravely resisted a sense of desolation.

"Now what?" she thought and drove her buggy into her own yard, turned it over to Luther, and entered a house more empty than she could have imagined.

32

Meg looked down at her hands, clasped together in her lap. She glanced at Royce, nearby on the fallen log; his gaze was fixed on some distant point just over the horizon.

Quite a scene for a proposal, she thought wryly. Where was the bended knee? Where the impassioned words? the tender looks?

But then, Meg had the honesty to admit, I've never pretended, even to myself, that I had a great passion for Royce. No, not even a small one, she recognized now with some surprise. Why should she expect more of him?

It had seemed enough, in the beginning, that she find a way West. Perhaps it was because of her recent prayers about the whole matter, but she felt a certain sense of shame now for her less than acceptable motive. How unfair she had been to Royce; he deserved better (though, to be *thoroughly* honest, she didn't think that was Marlys).

Royce was waiting for her answer. The situation, as far as she could see, was the same as it was in Toronto: Royce wanting a wife; she, Meg, wanting to live in the West.

Why did she hesitate? Was it because Royce deserved better? Probably not, she admitted, not proud of it. And suddenly her own bereft, empty heart cried out, "*I* deserve better!"

I need someone, she pursued, her thoughts weaving just as painfully as the fingers she was twisting in her lap, *someone to love, wholeheartedly!*

Love . . . the word seemed to catapult her heart into action.

Without the permission of her mind, her heart spoke, and the revelation it made stunned her. Her heart, without the permission of her head, had gone about its business and quietly, artfully, cunningly, and surely made its decision and choice and given itself away. It was no longer her own; it had pledged itself to another.

Now—that willful heart, bent on having its own way— beat in her breast like a moth seeking entrance to the light and an escape from the dark secrecy to which she had consigned it.

Be still! Be silent! her head now commanded. *What you have suggested is incredible . . . impossible!*

When the inner tumult had subsided, though not silenced, her head—that severe taskmaster—spoke. Spoke, she thought, as if it truly were in charge.

Do me the honor of marrying me, he had said.

"It would be an honor, Royce, a very great honor . . ." Meg's words fell into the well of silence between them and then faltered.

"But?" Royce, at last, swung his head to look at her.

"It doesn't seem quite . . . fair."

"Fair? To me, Meg, or to you?" The words were quiet but the tone intense.

"To you, of course . . ."

"Just me, Meg?" Royce pursued.

Meg's heart stirred again; and again her head, almost with panic, refused to hear what it was saying.

"Do you love me, Meg?" The silvery eyes seemed dark

now, pinning her with their persistence.

"I wanted," she said faintly, "to come West. I think . . . perhaps . . . it might have grown into . . . love, if . . ."

"I understand," Royce said quietly.

"You were looking for a wife," Meg spoke rapidly now, defensively, "and I was looking for a way West. It didn't seem a bad bargain . . . at the time. But I don't blame you," she added quickly, "for making a choice of the heart and not the head—" (*Be still, you betrayer, be still!* she ordered her own clamoring heart.)

Royce was silent.

Then, "I didn't think I had a choice," he said quietly.

Meg could only stare at him uncomprehendingly.

"How could any man ask a girl to give up her inheritance? Charged with that decision, what choice did I have?"

Meg's mind took a moment to grope through the unreality and untruth of what Royce had just revealed.

Then, "Marlys—" she said simply.

"It wasn't true, the limitations on the inheritance, was it?"

Meg drew a deep breath. So much was explained. Marlys had casually played with her sister's dreams and with a man's entire future. And had, all unwittingly, saved them both from making a terrible mistake.

"It doesn't matter anymore," she said quietly.

Royce saw it too. "Those prayers of Neal's . . . and yours," he said, and his smile came through the half-dark that had fallen, "I suppose we should both be grateful for them.

"What will you do, Meg?" Royce asked. "I hope you'll stay on. And for," his voice had the persistent tone he had used when he had probed to see if she loved him, "a better reason."

Meg looked at him, startled. Had her traitorous heart betrayed her, without her knowledge?

"But he . . . Neal," she whispered, honest at last, "has urged me . . . pushed me . . . gently, of course, in your direction."

Royce's voice was filled with affection. "What a loyal brother he is! Can you suppose I'm not as caring about him as he is about me? As long as he thought you and I—that is, I'm quite sure he'll light up like the aurora borealis when we get back and tell them our decision."

And he did. Not knowing it, Neal's indrawn breath and lit eyes spoke volumes to the brother who knew him so well and loved him so much, and the girl who knew him only a little and loved what she knew.

There was some laughter as the group examined the abortive love affair, much lightheartedness as they sat down to a fresh cup of tea. If the first flush of joy on Neal's face quickly changed to a troubled thoughtfulness, it went unnoticed.

Later, preparing for bed, Becky said dolefully, "I hope this doesn't mean you aren't going to stay, Meggie."

Perhaps it was stubbornness, perhaps it was embarrassment for her earlier conniving to be the wife of a homesteader, but Meg determined now to go home.

"I think I better go back to Toronto, Becky," she said quietly and blew out the light.

In the morning, while Becky prepared breakfast, Meg packed. Royce watched speculatively, Neal uneasily, Becky was just plain outraged. "Why? Things are going along just great here!"

"Royce needs to be back in his own house," Meg said lamely. "He and Neal can't share one place forever. And now," she said, pinning on her hat, "will you take me to the train . . . Royce?" Meg looked pointedly at Royce.

"Sorry, I've got fencing to do. Neal will have to take you," Royce said firmly.

With a pale face and pounding heart, Meg climbed into the buggy, having received a tearful, reluctant farewell from Becky.

It seemed that Neal and Meg—always before able to engage in easy camaraderie—could find nothing to say to each other.

"I understand why you're leaving," Neal said in a rather hollow tone. "It wouldn't be pleasant—staying around a man who, though he had the chance, didn't want you."

"But it wasn't—"

"You deserve to be a man's *first* choice!" Neal's usually gentle face was flushed, and he jerked the innocent horse's mouth with some fierceness.

The horse curvetted, and Meg held on for dear life, unable at the moment to respond to Neal's surprising reaction. Neal, obviously, didn't understand. Didn't understand at all.

"Royce didn't . . . didn't share with you . . ." Meg faltered.

"He just said you'd be the best one to tell me." Neal's bronzed jaw tightened. "Last night—you both laughed and tried to act as if . . . well, I know your heart must have been broken!"

In spite of herself, Meg laughed. It was such a joyous sound, spilling over the surrounding bush, that it rivaled the ever-present birdsong. And it caused Neal to turn and look at her with eyes in which comprehension was beginning to dawn.

"Whoa!" Neal pulled the horse to a halt there on the lonely country road.

"Look at me, Meg," he ordered, his misery, borne of despair, only beginning to subside. Meg, of course, was already looking. Looking into gray eyes that had, unknown to her (except to her independently acting heart), grown very dear. Seeing and recognizing the hope that dawned in them took her breath away, and her own face, growing equally as expressive, spoke what her lips had not yet learned to say.

"Is it possible—?" Neal asked, wonderingly.

Meg's untutored heart prompted her lips to confess, though quaveringly, "I've never been in love . . . before."

All the hopes, all the dreams, all the expectations of each of them found fulfillment in the arms that reached and took and held.

The mare, sensing the free reins, moved to the grass beside the road and munched at will. A butterfly, lighting on the dash and lingering safely, palpitated in somewhat the same rhythm as the two nearby human hearts.

Eventually Neal and Meg drew apart, holding hands and gazing into each other's eyes, lost in the wonder of love between a man and a woman. Where had it come from! God, surely.

So this, Meg thought bemusedly, *is how it's supposed to be,* and wondered how she had thought she could settle for less.

"You can't go back to Toronto," Neal said and Meg agreed. But neither did she feel good about turning around, driving back into the Ferguson yard, and announcing, "Well, here I am again!"

"But you'd like a little time—" Neal said, correctly interpreting the uncertainty in Meg's starry eyes.

"It isn't that I don't know . . . for sure," Meg said, though a little shyly. "It just seems that it might be wise to let a little time go by. Harley," she laughed, "is going to be so confused. Perhaps he can come and give me away . . . by Christmas."

She had to have a kiss for her wisdom. He must have one for his understanding.

"I have the perfect solution," Neal said when conversation seemed the sensible thing to do. "You shall stay with Miss P."

"Miss P? I've heard of her, of course. Are you sure—?"

"Positive! She'll welcome you with open arms. In fact, she'll see you as a godsend. But be prepared," Neal advised solemnly, clucking to the horse and taking up the reins, "for a running study of the Bible."

"Well, then," the willing student responded, "it won't be wasted time after all."

And the buggy swayed on down the road—the two figures on the spring seat blending almost as one—to the small home where Miss Partridge was about to have her next assignment thrust upon her, in a complete reversal of the scripture, "Go out into the highways and hedges, and compel them to come in."